$\Upsilon(\Gamma)$ $\overline{A?}$

Bass Reeves

In 1875, the notorious Judge Parker commissioned fifty black deputy marshals to keep the peace in Indian Territory, the most untamed area of the West. To bring order into the Territory these men must cross the 'deadline', a railroad which marks the boundary between civilization and lawlessness.

Unique amongst these brave men is Bass Reeves, who sets himself apart by his untiring devotion to justice and deadly skills with a gun. But when his own son, Benny, is accused of murder and flees into the Territory, Bass is forced to question everything for which he has stood.

Now he has to ride across the deadline with Benny's arrest warrant and is forced to find out which is stronger: blood or law.

Bass Reeves

ADAM WRIGHT

A Black Horse Western

ROBERT HALE · LONDON

ISBN 0 7090 6983 9

Robert Hale Limited
Clerkenwell House
Clerkenwell Green
London EC1R 0HT

To Lynne, with all my love

Typeset by
Derek Doyle & Associates, Liverpool.
Printed and bound in Great Britain by
Antony Rowe Limited, Wiltshire

Acknowledgements

Special thanks to Art T. Burton of Columbia College, Chicago for sharing his research on Bass Reeves. Art is the author of 'Black, Red and Deadly' (Eakin Press, Texas) and 'Black, Buckskin and Blue' (Eakin, Texas) and provided me with the fragments of Bass's life history that are woven into this story.

Bass Reeves was a unique character. Absolutely fearless, and knowing no master but duty. The placing of a writ in his hands for service meant that the letter of the law would be fulfilled though his life paid the penalty.

Muskogee Phoenix, 12 January 1910

Foreword

In 1875, Judge Isaac Parker ('The Hanging Judge') was appointed to bring law and order to the Indian Territory north of Texas. This huge area of America's West served as a haven for thieves, rustlers and murderers. It also provided a home for many Indian tribes.

Because of the Indians' mistrust of white men, Parker commissioned fifty black US Deputy Marshals to keep the peace in this dangerous region. One of these men, Bass Reeves, arrested 3,000 outlaws during his career, putting fourteen notches on his gun in the process.

Reeves was one of the few men who dared to cross the 'deadline', the MK&T (Missouri, Kansas & Texas) Railroad line which ran through Oklahoma and marked the boundary of western civilization. The outlaws who escaped into Indian Territory left posters along the railroad, attesting that death awaited any lawman who crossed the line. Bass saw these taunts as a challenge.

But his desire for justice and skill with a gun soon forced him to cross another line. The line between law and blood. . . .

One

Although he was tired by the time he reached Wild Horse Creek, Bass Reeves knew he had to keep his wits about him. He slowed his horse to a trot as he rode through the trees. The animal darted its head back and forth, as if sensing his wariness.

He squinted against the dull dusk light, his senses on edge. The townsfolk at Marysville had told him that Daniel Evans and William Spivey had fled this way after learning that Judge Parker had issued writs for their arrest. Those writs sat among the thick wad of papers in Bass's saddle-bag, and the crimes listed on them included horse theft and murder.

He dismounted, stood stock-still, and listened. The creek gurgled somewhere in the distance and birds chattered noisily in the trees, but that was all. Bass unbuttoned his long coat and swept it behind his twin holsters. His Colts sat butt-forward in his belt, facilitating a quick draw.

He tied the horse to a tall tree, retrieved two pairs of handcuffs from his saddle-bag then edged forward towards the creek. A cool breeze whispered through the trees.

By the time he reached the shallow creek, he heard voices carried on that breeze.

The clear water tumbled over mossy rocks and fallen trees, chuckling to itself as it raced to join the Red River to the south. Bass knelt on the dirt bank and listened to the indistinct voices, gauging their source.

The trees on the far side of the creek.

He took a careful step into the water, keeping hold of a low branch until his footing on the slippery rocks was sure. He felt exposed here, but he resisted the temptation to rush across to the opposite bank. Too much noise, too easy to slip.

The water rushed just below the tops of his high boots as he walked across the creek. He pulled the Colts from their holsters and held them at hip level, partly to aid his balance, but also because he knew that Evans and Spivey would kill him to evade the law that he represented. They knew that if they were taken to Fort Smith, they would hang for sure. Judge Parker was famous for meting out harsh justice to criminals, and his tool for that justice was the noose.

Bass reached the bank and stepped out of the water. The voices were clearer now. He still couldn't make out any words but the conversation sounded relaxed. That was good. They didn't know he was there.

He followed the creek north, moving among the trees, crouching to avoid the low branches. After a couple of minutes creeping through the wood, he came upon his prey in a small clearing.

Daniel Evans. Tall and blond, dressed in a checked shirt and braces. He busied himself unsaddling his horse, a bay, while he spoke to Spivey.

Spivey was small, stout and dark. He sat on a fallen tree trunk, toying with a revolver. His horse, a pinto, stood unsaddled behind him. The saddle lay at Spivey's feet.

The fact that Spivey had a weapon in his hand unnerved Bass. Maybe he should wait until the men were asleep before walking into their camp. But he was tired and he wanted to get this over with. He had been on the trail for two months and once he had Evans and Spivey, he could return to Fort Smith, then home to Muskogee for a while.

His prison wagon, which he had left a couple of miles back with John Harjo (the Seminole Indian posse man Bass was mandated to take on official business), would be full when Evans and Spivey were caught. Full and ready for delivery to Fort Smith where Judge Parker's court would deal with the criminal occupants.

Bass levelled his Colts at the two men in the

clearing then stepped forward and said, 'You boys
gonna come quietly?'

Evans, standing by his horse, jumped with
shock as he heard Bass's voice, then pressed
himself against the saddle he had been untying.

'Get away from that saddle-bag,' Bass said
firmly. He waved the muzzle of one Colt at Evans
while he kept the other, and his eyes, trained on
Spivey. Armed, Spivey presented the greatest
threat.

'Drop the revolver, Spivey.'

Spivey looked at the revolver in his hand, then
at Bass. 'Goddamn judge sent a black man after
us, Bill,' he said to Evans. 'You here to arrest us
or kill us, black man?'

'Name's Reeves,' Bass said. He nodded at the
tin star pinned to his coat. 'Deputy US Marshal
Reeves.'

'Bass Reeves?' Evans asked.

Bass watched Evans with his peripheral vision
while he kept his attention focused on Spivey and
the revolver in his hand. 'That's me,' he said.

Evans put up his hands and moved away from
the horse. 'I'll come quiet.'

'What the hell you doing?' Spivey shouted at
his partner. 'We got nothing to fear from this guy!'

'I'd drop that iron if I was you, Bill,' Evans said,
his eyes darting from Bass to the revolver in
Spivey's hand. 'I heard of this guy. They don't let
him shoot in turkey shoot contests no more on

14

account of he's too good a shot.'

Spivey sneered. 'I ain't no turkey.'

'Do as your friend says,' Bass suggested. 'Drop the iron and let's go.' He kept his eyes fixed on the revolver in Spivey's hand, waiting for the slightest movement.

Spivey seemed to consider the situation for a moment. He looked at Bass's Colt pistols, at Evans standing with his hands in the air, then at his own gun. He stood up.

This is it, Bass thought, he's gonna go for me.

'I ain't going to hell with no noose round my neck,' Spivey said. He brought the gun up, thumbing back the hammer.

Bass squeezed the Colt's trigger and the *boom* shattered the dusk quiet of the woods. William Spivey spun to his right like a demented dancer, the gun in his hand discharging uselessly at the ground. Spivey landed on his back, groaning.

Evans had a sudden change of heart and made a play for his own gun. The Colt in Bass's right hand spoke once, sending Evans stumbling backwards into the trees.

Bass strode over to the moaning Spivey, cocking one Colt as he slid the other into his gunbelt. With his free hand, he retrieved a pair of handcuffs from his pants' pocket and roughly cuffed Spivey's hands behind his back. Blood stained the right side of the outlaw's shirt and he cried out as Bass drew his right arm back.

15

Evans was dead. He lay staring at the darkening sky but seeing nothing. Bass cinched the saddle Evans had been untying, then heaved the body across it. He saddled Spivey's horse, threw the protesting man over the saddle, then grabbed both sets of reins and headed back towards the creek.

'You crazy bastard!' Spivey shouted from his horse as they reached the creek. 'Don't you read the posters we leave along the railroad? Any lawman crossing the deadline is gonna get killed sooner or later.'

Bass stopped and turned around to face him. 'Is that what those posters say?' He shook his head, feigning astonishment. 'Maybe it's time I learned to read.'

As he led the horses and the protesting outlaw across the creek, Bass laughed into the night.

TWO

As he guided the horses towards the prison wagon nestled in the woods, Bass was glad to see that John Harjo had lit a campfire. The chill of the night had crept into Bass's joints during the ride back from the creek.

He dismounted and nodded a greeting to the Seminole Indian. Harjo sat by the fire, dressed in a blue chequered shirt and brown pants held up by braces. The flickering glow from the flames played over his wide face and the rifle resting across his knees, He nodded back to Bass then pointed at the wagon. 'They been a bit noisy tonight.'

Bass glanced at the covered wagon. There were five men inside, chained to the iron bar that ran along the floor. 'They sound quiet enough now.' He started to unsaddle his horse.

Harjo grinned then held up the butt of his rifle. 'Had to persuade a couple of 'em that it was bedtime. The others soon got the idea.'

17

Bass chuckled, set his saddle over a fallen branch, then went to check on Spivey. The outlaw had become quiet during the trip from the creek; probably resigned to his fate, Bass guessed. He unholstered a Colt, pointed it casually at Spivey. 'OK, get down.'

Spivey shot a dark look at Bass then slid from the saddle. He stood looking at the ground, hands cuffed behind him.

Bass gestured to the wagon with his gun. 'Move.'

Spivey looked at the prison wagon then back at Bass. 'When are you gonna unchain me, Reeves?'

'Those chains come off when you get to Fort Smith,' Bass said. 'Now get over to the wagon.'

Spivey dawdled across to the wagon, head bowed. Bass wasn't sure if the outlaw was defeated, or if his complacency was a trick. He nodded at Harjo. 'Keep him covered for me, John, while I open the wagon up.'

Harjo got up from the fireside and levelled his rifle at Spivey.

The law officers at Fort Smith had fitted the wagon with a hinged, wooden, lockable door. Bass fished the key out of his pocket and unlocked it. Although the men inside were all chained, he steadied his Colt as he let the door drop. These men were dangerous.

The five occupants lay quietly in the dark wagon interior, chains from their wrists securing them to the central iron bar. 'Get in,' Bass said to Spivey.

The outlaw complied, climbing sullenly into the wagon. Harjo came up beside Bass, his rifle sights still pointed at Spivey. Bass unlocked one cuff from the outlaw's wrist then attached it to the wagon's bar. 'I ain't no animal,' Spivey moaned.

'No,' Bass said. 'You're a killer.' He closed the wagon door and locked it. 'And you keep quiet in there with your new friends. Maybe reflect some on what damage you've been causing to decent people.' He walked back to the fire with Harjo.

They sat in the warm glow and Bass said, 'We should reach Fort Smith tomorrow.'

Harjo nodded. 'I can't wait to taste real home cooking again. Elly makes great pot roast.'

Bass laughed. 'Better than yours, anyway, John. You married the right girl, there. It's better that you don't cook. Your kids would never survive.'

'You been eating my cooking all this time,' Harjo said.

'Yeah, and I'm a big strong man. And I *still* get gutrot from your food.'

Harjo laughed. He settled back against a tree trunk and Bass did the same, feeling weariness wash over him.

'One thing I'm looking forward to,' Bass said, 'is Jenny's apple pie. She makes a real great pie, crammed full of apples.' He closed his eyes, remembering the day before he had set out on the trail. Jenny had baked an apple pie that day and they had sat at the kitchen table eating and laughing. The day had been a good one.

Until Benny had turned up, drunk.

'I need to make sure my boy's OK when I get back to Muskogee,' Bass told Harjo.

'Benny?' the Indian asked. 'He still having trouble with his woman?'

'Yeah,' Bass said, staring into the orange flicker of the fire. 'The day before I left, he came to the house. He was drunk and he was cursing Mary Lou, saying that she was a whore and that she'd got herself a lover. Benny always did have a quick temper, but that day, he was so fired up, he scared Jenny.'

'Well, if his wife is fooling around,' Harjo said, 'I can see why he's mad about it.'

Bass nodded, watching the flames burn low. 'I just hope the boy doesn't let that temper run away with him and do something stupid.' He threw a log on to the fire. As it landed, sparks exploded into the night like an angry swarm of fireflies.

'The thing I miss most being out here,' Harjo said as he shifted against the tree trunk, 'is sleeping in a proper bed.'

Bass shrugged. 'Ain't nothing wrong with being on the trail. Tell you the truth, John, I been on the trail most of my life and when I'm at home, I start to miss it.' He watched the flames consume the wood. 'When I'm home, I feel like I'm getting in Jenny's way, getting under her feet. The kitchen is her territory.' He gestured to the night around them. 'This is mine.'

The Indian remained silent for a moment then turned to Bass and said, 'It is an honourable job.'

'I don't know much about honour.' Bass watched the stars in the night sky, his eyes picking out patterns among the bright pinpricks of light. 'But I do know that this is the only job that makes sense to me. It's about doing what's right. Those men,' he gestured to the prison wagon, 'have all done wrong. They have to pay for that. So someone has to come across into this territory and find them. I'm good at that job because I believe in what I do. But I don't know anything about honour.'

'My people have a saying,' Harjo said. 'A man who follows righteousness along the trail will walk for many days. You will live a long and fruitful life.'

Bass laughed. 'I ain't following righteousness down any trail, John. If there is such a trail, then I was forced on to it long ago.' He watched the stars again, his thoughts passing back over the years to a poker game in a smoky saloon. 'Where I am today ain't because of any choice I made. It's because of the colour of my skin and a bad hand of cards.'

In the fireglow, he could see a frown crease Harjo's face.

'It was in Texas a long time ago,' Bass explained. 'There was a poker game that went on into the night. One of those long games where the stakes keep getting higher and the turn of the cards means everyone's nerves keep getting more and more frayed. You know what I mean?'

The Seminole shook his head.

'Well, the players in this game were mainly rich businessmen. A couple of guys from New York who were looking to buy land, three Texan ranchers, a banker from the east coast, and a landowner from Missouri.'

He threw another log on to the fire and watched the sparks scatter into the night. 'The cards ran bad for the landowner. Every hand he played, every call he made, went wrong. He'd inherited his business while he was still young, so he had youth and power and the quick temper of a kid. That is a dangerous combination in a high-stakes card game. I could see the anger rising in him after each hand. He watched his money going to the other men and he decided to strike out at the nearest thing to hand. And the nearest thing to hand was me.'

Bass watched the images flicker over his inner eye. He remembered the card game as if it was yesterday, although it had been twenty years ago. He remembered it so vividly because that poker game had changed his life.

'He had a bull whip next to his chair,' he told Harjo. 'He had a gun too, of course, but it was the whip he went for. First I knew of it was when I felt a sting across my shoulders. The pain and the shock sent me crashing out of my chair and to the floor. Then he was on me, whip squeezed tight in one hand while he used the thick handle like a club. I got hit around the head a couple times before I started getting real scared. He wasn't going to stop until he busted the whip or my head. I could see that in his eyes.' He paused, drew in a deep breath of air. Even now, the memory affected him, made his heart race in his chest, brought out a cold sweat from his skin.

'What about the others?' Harjo asked. 'Didn't they try to stop him?'

Bass laughed lightly. 'It wasn't their place, John. Just like it wasn't my place to do what I did next.'

'What do you mean? If he was—'

Bass held up a hand, silencing his partner. 'I'll come to that in a minute. Everyone in the saloon was watching by now but no one could do anything to stop the son of a bitch from killing me. So I did the only thing I could, the one thing that went against everything I had ever been taught.' He watched the bright stars moving across the night sky, fulfilling their destinies. 'I struck back.'

'You'd been taught *not* to stand up for your-self?'

'In this situation, yes. But I reached out and I grabbed the whip handle as it came rushing toward my face. The landowner stopped dead in his tracks and his eyes went wide as wagon wheels. I stood up, still holding the whip. I was a lot taller than he was and he seemed to shrink as I got to my feet. Everyone else must have caught a dose of his surprise because the whole place went quiet. Then the landowner tried to hit me again, with his fists this time. I wasn't having none of it, though.' He closed his eyes and watched the mental images flicker across his mind.

'I hit him square in the jaw and he went down. I should have left it at that, I guess. But by now the anger inside me had started boiling and I jumped on him and started pounding at him with my fists.' Bass opened his eyes and held his big hands out, clenching and unclenching them. His palms were sweaty. 'Folk started grabbing me and trying to pull me off him but I didn't notice. I just kept pounding and pounding.' He closed his eyes again.

'There was blood. Lots of it. Mine and his. And suddenly I got scared. I could see that the landowner was beaten up real bad. He lay there with his face all bloody and he was groaning in pain. I got up and ran. Someone tried to shoot me

24

as I got to the saloon doors but the bullet just winged the doorframe. Then I was in the street. Free. I escaped across the border into Mexico and all the while I vowed that I would return and devote my life to stopping the men who hurt others. The men who break the law. The men who kill others for no reason other than personal gain.'

'This man who beat you,' Harjo said. 'He was a wicked man.'

'Yes,' Bass said. He hunkered down against the tree and pulled a blanket over his body. The night had turned suddenly cold.

'But there is something that puzzles me.'

'What's that?'

'You said that fighting back against this wicked man went against your teaching. And you said that you are walking this trail because of a bad hand of cards and the colour of your skin.'

'Yes.'

'I do not understand.'

'It's simple really,' Bass said. 'That landowner was my master.' He pulled the blanket up to his neck and settled himself on the forest floor. 'And I was his slave.'

Three

They rode into the town of Fort Smith by late afternoon of the following day. Harjo steered the prison wagon through the main street, heading for the fort that gave the town its name.

Bass rode alongside, anxious to unload his prisoners then ride on to Muskogee to see Jenny and the kids. He worried about Benny's marriage and knew that he had to have a talk with the boy. If Mary Lou was seeing someone else then maybe Benny should think about getting a petition for divorce. He was a highly-strung boy with a rattlesnake temper. Mix that with a two-timing wife and the result could be dangerous.

The soldiers at the fort opened the gate when they saw the prison wagon and Harjo drove it into the dusty fort compound. Bass dismounted and tied his horse to a hitching rail outside Isaac Parker's courthouse. 'You get the horses watered and cleaned and I'll find the Marshal,' he told Harjo.

He strode through the glass-panelled door of the US marshal's office and into the reception area. The room was small, containing only a desk, the door to US Marshal Leo Bennett's office, and Nelly Harper, Bennett's secretary. As Bass closed the door behind him, she looked up and her eyes widened with surprise.

Nelly was in her fifties, with her grey hair scraped back into a tight bun. She had worked at the fort for as long as Bass could remember, taking messages, writing letters and sending telegrams on the machine which sat in the corner of the room. Her husband had been killed in the war and she had thrown herself into her job for the marshal wholeheartedly since his death. She wore small round spectacles. And behind those spectacles, her grey eyes continued to widen.

'Mr Reeves . . . I. . . .'

'Hello, Nelly. Everything OK?'

'Well, yes, that is . . . well. . . .' She fumbled with some papers on her desk, spilling a pile of letters on to the floor. Bass bent to retrieve them.

'You all right, Nelly?' The marshal's secretary was normally calm and efficient.

She nodded and a strand of hair whipped loose from the bun behind her head. 'Have you . . . have you seen Marshal Bennett yet?'

'Erm, no, ma'am. That's why I'm here. Got a wagon-load of prisoners outside and I need some new warrants.' He replaced the letters on her desk.

'Of course,' she said. 'Mr Bennett is in his office. Go right in.'

Bass started for the door but she stopped him with a hand on his arm. He looked down at her and she said, 'Mr Reeves, I'm so sorry.'

He frowned. 'Sorry for what?'

She gestured to Bennett's door.

Bass knocked once on the door then entered the office. US Marshal Leo Bennett sat reclining in his big leather chair, feet on his desk. He puffed smoke from a pipe clamped between his lips, adding to the lingering stink of tobacco in the office. Leo was a big man but in a stocky sort of way. His meaty arms looked powerful beneath his shirt and his chest was solid as a side of beef. His powerful physique belied his age, which Bass guessed was sixty at least. Leo's hair had gone white a long time ago, and only his moustache held a few remnants of dark hair. He sat up when he saw Bass.

'Good to see you, Bass,' he said around the pipe. 'Take a seat.' He gestured to a chair in front of his wide desk and lay the smoking pipe in an ashtray.

Bass sat and surveyed the office. He liked Leo's office but often wondered how a man as fit as Leo could choose to work among bookshelves, desks, papers and documents and not outside in the sunshine. He would go crazy if he had to work in an office all day.

'So tell me, Bass. How are you feeling? It's a sad business.' Leo shook his head and took another puff on the pipe. 'A sad business.'

Bass felt a hollowness in his gut. 'Leo, has something happened? Nelly acted strange when she saw me and now. . . .'

Leo slammed the pipe back into the ashtray. 'You mean you don't know? Haven't you spoken with anyone since you came in?'

Bass shook his head. 'No, I came straight here. I got a wagon full of prisoners out there.'

'I thought someone would have said something to you. Whole fort's been buzzing with the news, wondering when you'd get back off the trail.'

Bass stood, scraping the chair back along the wooden floor. 'What is it? Is it Jenny?' A sudden anxiety spread through him. If anything had happened to Jenny. . . .

Leo held up a big hand. 'No, Bass. Sit down. Jenny's fine.' He searched through some papers on his desk, located what he was looking for, and sighed. 'It's this.'

He handed Bass an arrest warrant.

Bass looked at the name scrawled on the warrant then shrugged. 'You know I can't read, Leo.'

The marshal nodded then pointed to the paper. 'Bass, the name written on that warrant is Benjamin Reeves.'

Bass felt his hands shaking. The paper quivered in his fingers so he set it on the desk. 'That stupid boy,' he said.

Leo said softly, 'I'm sorry.'

'When?'

'Last week. From the report, it seems Benny had a fight with Mary Lou. A hell of a fight. Neighbours found her body.'

'And Benny?'

Leo shrugged. 'He's gone. Lit out. That warrant has been sitting on my desk for a week. I've been trying to give it to my best deputies but no one wants to take the case, seeing how he's your son. Even Deputies Wood and Wright refused the case, and they usually take any dirty job that comes along.'

Bass stood and moved to the window. He looked out across the fort compound. Harjo and a group of soldiers unloaded the wagon, leading the shackled prisoners by gunpoint to the jailhouse to await sentencing. Those men, the men Bass had tracked and captured, were murderers. And now Benny, who Bass had seen born into this world and loved from that day, was a murderer as well.

'Give me the writ,' he said to the marshal.

'Bass, are you sure? With him being your son and all, it might not be a good idea. I can talk to Wood and Wright again, persuade them. . . .'

'No. I'll take the case.' He strode back to the desk, picked up the arrest warrant and folded it into his pocket. 'I need to go to Muskogee and see Jenny, then I'll go after him.'

Leo picked up the pipe and sucked on it but it was now dead. He replaced it in the ashtray. 'And when you find him? What will you do then?'

Bass turned to the door. 'My job.'

Four

The small town of Muskogee brought back fond memories for Bass as he rode towards his house. It was in this town that he had met and married Jenny and started their family. He was well known here and felt free of the discrimination he often encountered elsewhere. Throughout his years of chasing criminals in dangerous Indian territory and risking his life, Muskogee had remained a constant haven, a place of stability and familial warmth.

But now that warmth had been tainted by murder. A mixture of anger and sadness rested in Bass's gut like a cold, coiled snake.

He rode along the main drag to the livery barn where Jud Sanders housed Bass's horses for free. Sanders flatly refused payment but kept his horses in such fine condition that Jenny regularly supplied the widower with home-cooked meals.

Bass dismounted outside the barn and Jud came hobbling up to him. 'A terrible thing, Bass,' he said, shaking his head.

Bass nodded and handed the reins to the old man.

'Folks at the fort been panicking over who's gonna go get your boy. Decided to wait till you got back.' He shook his head again and stared at the horizon, where the sun lay low over the hills and bathed them a bloody red. ' 'Course, I told everyone that no one had better go after Benny except yourself. He's your boy and I guess that makes it your right to bring him in. You *are* gonna go after him yourself, ain't ya?'

'Yeah,' Bass said. 'Like you say, he's my boy. Are my other horses OK?'

Jud nodded. 'Yes, sir. Those greys of yours are strong beasts. I guess you'll be needing one of 'em saddled up?'

'Tomorrow, Jud. I need to see Jenny and find out exactly what happened before I go off half-cocked. I got a feeling inside me that's like rage and despair at the same time and I don't want to go doing nothing rash. I always work my job according to a routine and I can't change that now just because my family is involved.' He thanked the old man then set off on foot towards his home.

The townsfolk greeted Bass with hesitant nods of the head, some avoiding his eyes, and Bass felt saddened by the fact that his family, who had been known for upholding the law, were now connected with murder. As he approached his neighbourhood, his heart lifted slightly with the thought of seeing Jenny again after so long on the trail.

He opened the small gate to the house and looked up. Jenny stood there in the doorway, tears in her eyes. 'Oh, Bass,' she said, then ran to him. He held her close, enjoying the feel of her soft, lithe body and the light scent of soap on her skin.

They embraced in the light of the dying sun then Jenny said, 'Come on, supper's ready.' She led him into the house and to the kitchen.

'Pa's home!' Alice came running up to Bass, accompanied by her brother, Bass Jnr.

Bass held them tight then said, 'OK, sit down now.'

They sat at the table while Jenny served chicken and sweet potatoes. Bass wolfed the meal down, relishing the taste of Jenny's cooking and realizing just how much he had missed it while on the trail.

And tomorrow, he would be on the trail again – but under an entirely different set of circumstances.

He looked at his wife. Her skin was the colour of strong coffee, her face beautiful and framed by long black hair. She ate slowly and Bass could tell by the worried expression on her face that her mind was on Benny. He looked at Alice and Bass Jnr as they ate. At six and eight, they looked so innocent, just as Benny had at their age.

Bass ate in silence, his thoughts turning to the trail tomorrow.

Later, as he lay in bed with Jenny, the children asleep and the night silent, Bass watched the darkness beyond the window. Somewhere out there was his boy, running from justice – running from his father.

'Bass,' Jenny said. 'What's going to happen when you find him?'

Bass simply said, 'I'll bring him in.'

'And what's going to happen to him then?'

'That's up to the judge.'

He heard her sniff in the darkness. 'He's our boy.'

'He broke the law.'

'He's still our son.'

Bass reached out and touched her shoulder. 'He'll always be our son, Jenny. But Benny has committed murder. Think of poor Mary Lou.'

'I know,' she said. 'I know he has to be brought back. But I'm worried. How many men have you brought to Judge Parker?'

'Plenty. Too many to count.'

'And how many of those men have escaped the noose?'

'Some,' Bass said. But he knew that those few

36

men who had been sentenced to jail instead of the noose had been the exceptions. Judge Parker's lack of tolerance for criminals was well known.

Jenny lay her head on his chest. 'I'm worried for Benny.'

'So am I. But he has to be brought in. And it had better be me who finds him. There's a lot of guys with itchy trigger-fingers across the deadline.'

She looked up at him and even in the dark, he knew her dark eyes held a look of fear. 'Do you think he crossed into Indian territory?'

He nodded. 'They all run there sooner or later.'

'Benny is different from those other men.' Her voice held a trace of defiance.

'Is he?' Bass asked. 'You think those other men don't have parents who worry about them? You think they weren't innocent kids once?'

She remained silent for a few moments and Bass listened to the crickets chirping beyond the window.

Then Jenny said, 'Bass, when you find him, you'll look after our boy, won't you?'

He nodded and closed his eyes. Sleep crept up on him gradually then took him into a nightmare world of murder, betrayal and death.

Five

Morning brought a chill wind whispering down from the North. Bass, wrapped up in his duster and with his hat pressed firmly on his head, rode out of town to Benny's place. Dawn broke as he left Muskogee but the dull orange sunlight did nothing to warm the chill air. Nor did it lift the heavy sadness lodged in Bass's gut. Jenny had been tearful when Bass left the house earlier, and she had made him promise to bring Benny back safe and alive. Bass had nodded as he swung himself up into the saddle but he knew that Indian Territory was a deadly place. Beyond the deadline, life was as cheap as a bottle of rye.

He spotted Benny's place. The sight of the little white house with its back porch facing the rolling expanse of grassland brought back memories of happier days. Many times, he and Jenny had sat on that porch with Benny and Mary Lou, watching the sun setting over the plains, laughing,

39

drinking liquor, joshing each other. Mary Lou had baked wonderful pan bread.

And now she was dead.

Bass brought the horse to a halt and twisted in the saddle, fixing his gaze on the distant railroad track. The land beyond it was the haven of the meanest people ever to walk in this untamed country. Rustlers, thieves, murderers – and his son.

He slipped out of the creaking saddle and hitched his horse to the porch rail.

The morning was quiet and the house seemed eerily silent. Murder had been committed here, and to Bass it felt as if the house were holding its breath, waiting to exhale its secrets. He stepped on to the porch and his boots knocked loudly against the wood. He paused at the door, his fingers wrapped around the handle. He felt edgy.

Was it the atmosphere surrounding the house? Or was it something else?

He pulled one of the Colts from its holster and opened the door.

The entrance hallway was dark shadowy. Bass levelled the Colt and stepped over the threshold into the shadows. He stood still, listening. The house was silent.

Then he heard a sound from upstairs. A low keening from one of the bedrooms. A soft moan, full of anguish. Pulling his other Colt from its holster and holding both guns ahead of him, he ascended the stairs. The wood creaked beneath his boots and the moaning upstairs stopped.

Bass froze, listening. The bedroom door at the top of the staircase was shut, and Bass was sure the moaning had come from there. He heard a click, which he first took to be the door latch. He waited for the door to open. It didn't. He then realized the click had been the sound of a gun being cocked.

He thumbed back the hammers on his own guns. The double click cut through the quiet of the house. Whoever was behind the door must have heard it.

'Come out of there,' Bass called.

No answer.

'Unless you want trouble, open that door and come out peaceful. You got no business being in this house and I got two Colts waiting out here for you if you don't put your gun down.'

The voice from behind the door sounded furious. 'That you, Benny Reeves? You come back to gloat over what you did to poor Mary Lou? I'm coming out but I ain't putting my gun down. I'm gonna kill you, you bastard!'

The door flew open and crashed against the wall. A figure leapt out to the top of the stairs and Bass dropped to one knee. The man above him looked young and handsome in a dark, lean way but his eyes held a look of madness. Bass took all

41

of this in before the man fired. The revolver in his hand flashed and roared.

The bullet ripped into the banister by Bass's face. A splinter lodged itself painfully into his cheek. He raised the Colts simultaneously and squeezed the triggers. He was not aiming to kill. He wanted answers, and the only way he would get them would be to keep the man alive. But he had to shoot fast before his opponent got off a second, better-aimed, shot.

The twin Colts thundered in the enclosed space and the man tipped back into the bedroom. Bass bounded up the stairs, thumbing back the Colts' hammers as he reached the landing.

The man lay on his back next to the bed, groaning. An ugly red stain coloured his blue shirt near the right shoulder. The second bullet had punctured his left leg, just above the knee. The bloodstain there was smaller, like a budding red rose. The wounds didn't look serious.

Bass kicked the man's gun across the room and stood above him, the twin Colts aimed at his face. 'Who the hell are you and what are you doing in this house?'

The man struggled to get up, winced with pain, then lay back. 'Name's Bishell. Joe Bishell. I'm here because this is where the son of a bitch I'm chasing killed his wife.'

Bass frowned. 'You're a bounty hunter?'

Bishell shook his head and hatred flashed

across his face. 'This ain't about no bounty, mister.'

'Then what?'

'Vengeance. It ain't none of your concern so you let me up and I'll be on my way. That bastard's trail ain't cold yet.'

Bass leaned closer to Bishell's face and held the other man's gaze with his own. He pressed the cold steel of the Colt barrels against the other man's chin. 'This *is* my concern because the "bastard" you're talking about ain't no bastard. He's my son. And no one is going after him except me.'

Bishell's eyes travelled over Bass's face. 'So you're Bass Reeves.'

Bass nodded.

'Then you'll understand why I have to go after your son. He's a murderer, Mr Reeves, and he deserves justice.'

'He'll get it,' Bass said. 'When I find him.'

Bishell let out a short bark-like laugh. A sneer creased his handsome features. 'You think I believe that? He's your son.'

Bass nodded. 'And a murderer, as you say.' He stood and holstered the Colts.

'You'd kill your own son?'

'I said nothing about killing him.'

Bishell dragged himself to his feet then sat slumped on the bed. 'Killing is what he deserves.' A tear glided down his left cheek. 'An eye for an eye, the Bible says, doesn't it? After what he did to my Mary Lou. . . .'

Bass felt anger rise within him like a raging river. He grabbed Bishell's shirt and pulled the man to his feet. 'So you're the son of a bitch who destroyed my son's marriage.'

Bishell stared angrily. 'I didn't destroy nothing. Mary Lou was miserable with Benny. I showed her happiness. We loved each other. We were going to go north together, start a new life. . . .' He looked at the bed, then at the floor. 'And your son destroyed all that.' His gaze travelled to his gun. 'That's why I say killing's too good for him. He may be your son, Mr Reeves, but he doesn't have one ounce of the reputation you have.'

Bass let go of Bishell's shirt then moved to the door. He felt trapped in this house. The smell of death was too fresh in the air. Death and vengeance. He shot a look at Bishell and said, 'I'm going to find Benny and bring him back to the judge. Justice will be done, but it'll be done legal.'

Bishell remained silent and continued to stare at the gun on the floor.

'You aiming to follow my trail and try to handle things your own way?' Bass asked.

Bishell said nothing.

'I've hunted down and caught hundreds of men,' Bass said. 'Out of those hundreds, I've only killed twelve. I'm not a superstitious man,

Bishell, but I think thirteen could be an unlucky number for you.'

He strode out of the door and down the stairs. What had he hoped to gain by coming here? The house held nothing but dead memories. He unhitched his horse from the porch rail and spurred the animal back toward Muskogee. He felt like he was wasting time on this side of the deadline. He needed to be in Indian Territory as soon as possible. That was where Benny was.

He would call on John Harjo and cross the railroad before sundown.

As he rode toward his hometown, it struck him that he felt more at ease on the untamed side of the deadline than he did on the 'civilized' side. He brought the horse to a halt and shielded his eyes against the sun with one hand as he watched the railroad tracks. Beyond, the hills seemed dark even in the sunlight.

A white poster fluttered along the tracks, dancing in the breeze. Bass rode up to it, dismounted, then grabbed the paper. He could not read the words but he knew their meaning: death to any lawman who dared to cross the tracks.

He looked again at the dark hills. It would be safer to approach a nest of rattlesnakes than cross the deadline. Beyond the tracks, the land became a wild place of theft, rustling and murder.

The place where Bass belonged.

Six

John Harjo lived with his wife Elly in a small ranch house north of Muskogee. As Bass rode towards the property, he noticed Harjo working on a corral fence. He waved and the Indian waved back.

Bass dismounted, then adjusted the brim of his hat to shade his eyes from the bright midday sun. 'Nice work,' he said.

Harjo stood amongst a clutter of lumber, a tin pail of nails at his feet. He wore a blue shirt that was stained dark with sweat around his chest and arms. Beneath his hat, his long black hair was tied back into a ponytail and fixed with a feathered band.

Bass admired the fence, knowing that Harjo had erected it quickly yet efficiently. Quick and efficient were the powerful Indian's watchwords.

'There's still a lot of work to be done,' Harjo said, wiping his powerful arm across his forehead. 'Bass, I'm sorry about Benny.'

47

Bass nodded. 'I'm going after him, John. I want you to come with me.'

Harjo watched a bird pinwheel across the azure blue sky then looked at the ground. 'It is a sad day when a father must hunt down his own son. I know that you must do this, and I will help you. *Someone* has to watch over you in the badlands.'

Elly appeared on the porch with a pitcher of lemonade and the two men walked toward the house. Elly was a Seminole, the same as John, and she had inherited that race's native beauty. Her face was dark and pretty, her hair jet black and long. She wore a white blouse with blue piping and a light blue skirt. Like John, she favoured modern Western dress, yet her ethnic roots seemed to enhance her style rather than clash with it.

Bass smiled as they reached the porch. 'That lemonade sure looks good, Elly.'

She nodded then touched his shoulder gently. 'We're both sorry about Benny. I was going to call on Jenny later, do you think she would like that?'

'I'm sure she'd appreciate a visit, ma'am. Especially since I'll be leaving later today. I think she gets a little lonely sometimes.'

'You're leaving so soon?'

Bass took a sip of lemonade. It refreshed his parched throat, taking away the dry heat of the day. 'I have to go after my boy,' he said. 'I want to find him before anyone else does.'

'Of course. You must be out of your mind with worry.'

'I'll be going with him,' John said.

She frowned at her husband. 'But you only just got back. The fence. . . .'

'Can wait,' Harjo said. 'This is important. A friend in need of help is more important than a corral fence.'

Elly nodded. 'Of course. It's just that I'll miss you.' She turned to Bass. 'Look after my husband, won't you?'

'I always do,' Bass replied. 'If it wasn't for me looking after him on the trail and you looking after him at home, I don't know how he'd survive.'

'I know,' Elly said. 'He's so fragile.'

Harjo's laugh sounded deep and throaty, like a growling bear's. 'I could pick the both of you up above my head and still finish that fence.'

Bass finished his lemonade, chuckling. He remembered laughing and joking with Benny and Mary Lou like this. As those memories appeared in his head, he blocked them out.

Times had changed. Mary Lou was dead and Benny was a murderer. How will Benny react when I find him? Bass wondered. How will *I* react?

He thanked Elly for the lemonade then said, 'I have to get back to Muskogee and get ready to leave. John, meet me at the Old Wheel saloon before sundown. We'll cross the deadline tonight and make camp in the hills.'

Harjo nodded. He touched Bass's elbow lightly. 'Bass, I'm sure we'll find him and everything will be OK.' Bass smiled but there was no pleasure in it.

As he swung into the saddle, he thought to himself. If we find him, we bring him back to face the noose.

He tipped his hat to the Harjos and rode toward Muskogee. As he approached the town, a thought nagged him.

Which was the better death? The gun or the noose?

Seven

Jenny watched her husband pack his belongings into his saddle-bags. He sat at the kitchen table, busying himself with his preparations.

Jenny felt as she always did before Bass left for Indian Territory, proud and scared. She knew that he faced danger every day in his search for criminals, but she also felt a fierce pride in the fact that he was such a respected lawman.

As he fastened the buckles on the bags, she let her eyes pore over him, taking in every detail. She did this every time he left, committing him to memory. Because memories might soon be all she had left of him.

She refused to acknowledge that thought. In the beginning of Bass's career, she had wept when he was gone and she was alone in their bed. Now, she remembered the happy times they had spent together and she told herself that he would be home soon. He always returned. And he always left again.

She sometimes felt that the trail he rode in Indian Territory held more allure to him than his home life. He seemed edgy when he was at home, eager to return to the untamed hills across the deadline, to the way of the gun.

Her eyes widened slightly as she looked at the twin Colt pistols strapped to his belt. She would never get used to seeing those guns on her husband. To her and his children, he was as gentle as a soft summer breeze. The guns seemed incongruous with his character.

Yet she knew that rustlers and murderers feared this man she loved, and that he had used those guns in the course of his job. He had killed a dozen men.

Bass finished with the bags, sat back in his chair. He smiled thinly and said, 'It won't take us long to find him, Jenny.'

She nodded and attempted a weak smile. She thought of her son alone in Indian Territory and prayed that Bass found him quickly. But she also feared that the justice dealt to Benny would be in the form of a noose. 'Bass,' she said softly, voicing for the first time a thought that had sat in her mind for days. 'When you find him, do you have to bring him back here?'

He frowned then shrugged his powerful shoulders. 'What do you mean?'

'I mean, if you took him north, somewhere safe. If you left him somewhere where he could start a new life . . . would that be so bad?'

He stood. It was almost dark outside and the light from the table lamp cast his distorted shadow across the wall. In that moment, Jenny could understand why men feared him. His body was huge and powerfully muscled beneath his chequered shirt. His dark eyes held an inner strength that complemented his physical power. 'I can't do that,' he said. He turned and walked to the window. He watched the dusk envelop the fields behind the house.

Jenny stood and went to him, placing a hand tentatively on his big shoulder. 'I'm sorry,' she said, 'I shouldn't have. . . .'

'Do you think I haven't considered that myself? Do you think I want to bring Benny back here to be hanged?' She felt his body tremble beneath her touch.

'I don't know,' she admitted. 'Sometimes you seem to be driven by one thing only: the law. Bass, he's our son.'

He drew in a deep breath, then let it out in a sigh. 'I know that. I'm not angry because of what you said just now. I'm angry because I thought the same thing myself. It would be easy to find Benny, take him north all the way to Canada then turn him loose. That thought has nagged me since Leo Bennett gave me that writ.'

He turned to her and the strength in his eyes was gone, replaced by sadness and welling tears.

53

'But I can't do that,' he said. 'I can't think that. . . .'

'Why?' She herself would do anything to save Benny. Why couldn't Bass see that?

He sat at the kitchen table again, the chair creaking beneath his weight. 'Because if I do that then my entire life is a lie. I've brought all those men to justice because I believe that breaking the law is wrong. I still do. I can't change that belief just because it's Benny who's done something wrong. I can't turn a blind eye to murder.'

She understood what he meant. But her fear for Benny's future left a hollow pit in her stomach. 'You do what you have to do, Bass,' she said.

He stood up and hefted the saddle-bag over his shoulder. 'I will. I have to go, John will be waiting at the Old Wheel for me.' He strode for the door.

'Did you say goodbye to the children?' she asked.

He nodded. 'I told them I was leaving before they went to bed.' Leaning forward, he kissed her gently. Jenny wanted to hold him, to stop him from leaving, but she knew she must not. She could not.

Bass opened the door and stepped out into the gentle night breeze. 'I'll be back soon,' he promised.

She felt tears threatening. 'Just look after our boy.'

He nodded as he attached the saddle-bag to the

saddle of his horse. He walked back to her and kissed her cheek softly. 'Don't worry,' he whispered. He swung up on to the saddle then started to ride towards town.

Jenny watched him go, the sighing breeze drying his kiss on her cheek. By the time she got back into the house, the kiss was dry but her cheeks were wet with tears.

Eight

The Old Wheel saloon was normally a quiet place where hard-working men went to relax and drink. As Bass entered the room, though, he could sense a tension in the air.

At a table in the corner, near the fireplace, sat a group of men who were known in Muskogee as local hardcases. Minor run-ins with the law and cases of public disorder (usually drunken) had made their faces known to the townsfolk. Bass recognized Al Block, a huge, bearded bear of a man, and his younger and thinner brother Harry. Sitting next to Harry Block was Ned Stringer, a wiry wanderer who had settled in Muskogee some years back. And sitting next to Stringer was a man Bass recognized but had only recently met. Joe Bishell. The man's right shoulder was bandaged from his earlier wound but otherwise he seemed to harbour the same anger he had when Bass had first seen him.

The four men watched Bass as he walked to the bar. He felt their eyes burning into him as he ordered a whiskey. Once he had the drink in hand, he turned and leant against the bar, watching the other drinkers with disinterest. Out of the corner of his eye, he watched Bishell's table for any sudden movement.

The four remained quiet, speaking to each other in hushed tones while they watched Bass. An edge of nervous expectancy cut the smoky air.

Bass sipped the whiskey, felt it burn down his throat then replaced the glass on the scarred wooden surface of the bar. He beckoned Frank, the bartender, over with a jerk of his head.

'You want another drink already, Bass?' Frank asked.

Bass shook his head. 'Do something for me, Frank?' He spoke low, his eyes on Bishell's table and the four armed men sitting at it.

'Of course,' the bartender replied.

'Go get Sheriff Thomas.'

Frank hesitated then said, 'But there ain't no trouble.'

'There's gonna be.'

'OK, OK.' Frank disappeared behind the bar.

Bass wondered where Harjo was. He was late. Four against two was better odds than four against one. Maybe if Frank found the sheriff in time. . . .

Bishell stood up from the table, swaying

slightly. He pointed at Bass. 'That man,' he said, slurring his words, 'is perverting the course of justice.' The other drinkers turned to look at Bishell's table. Recognizing the faces of the Block brothers and Ned Stringer, they set down their drinks and left the saloon. Better to be somewhere else when trouble erupted between armed men.

'Sit down, Bishell,' Bass said. He felt strangely calm. The tense anticipation was gone, replaced by a heightened awareness, a sharpening of his senses. The saloon's pungent smoke-and-alcohol smell seemed stronger, the smoothness of the Colts' grips beneath his light touch felt like glass. His nerves tingled.

'Reeves,' Bishell said, staggering closer, 'you are a disgrace to your badge.' He got close enough for Bass to smell the liquor on his breath. 'Your own son is a killer and you're letting him get away.'

'I told you,' Bass said. 'I ain't letting anyone get away.'

Bishell snorted. 'We can't believe that can we, boys?'

The Block brothers and Stringer stood up. They didn't look drunk like Bishell, which made them more dangerous if they went for their guns.

'We're going after that boy of yours,' Bishell said. 'We're gonna make sure he pays for what he did to Mary Lou. Show him Ned.'

Ned Stringer reached under the table then held up a noose, grinning at Bass as he held it high.

'That's what your boy's got coming,' Bishell said, 'And I'm gonna watch him twisting on that rope.'

Bass struck out. His fist connected with Bishell's jaw and sent him sprawling across the saloon, colliding with tables and chairs as he stumbled to the floor.

Al Block stepped forward, his speed belying his size. Before Bass could reach his gun to warn the man off, Block had him in a bear hug. Bass felt his ribs and lungs constrict. He gasped for breath. Block tightened his grip.

Ned Stringer and Harry Block laughed as Al continued to squeeze the life out of Bass. Bass felt light-headed. Stars popped in his vision. He summoned the last of his strength to kick out. He raised his knee sharply into Block's groin. The big man released his grip then staggered backwards, gasping in pain.

Ned and Harry went for their guns. Bass went for his.

He flicked the Colts from their holsters and fired the two guns simultaneously. Ned yelped and went down, holding his hand. Harry Block dived for cover behind the table, dropping his gun as he hit the floorboards. He raised his hands over his head. 'OK, OK, I don't want no trouble.'

60

The saloon door opened and Bass whirled, expecting another attack.

Sheriff Thomas entered, his lean face registering surprise and amusement at the scene before him. Al Block lay on the floor clutching his groin. Joe Bishell lay unconscious among a litter of broken chairs. Ned Stringer sat nursing his bleeding hand, and Harry Block lay on his stomach, his arms still raised above his head.

The sheriff stroked his dark beard. 'Looks I came just in time to help, Bass.'

Bass laughed but there was no mirth in it. He still felt angry at Bishell's words. Why didn't anyone believe he was going to do the right thing when he found Benny? Did his reputation as a lawman mean so little that everyone assumed he would break the law for his son?

'I'd be obliged if you could keep these men in your cells overnight, Sheriff.'

Thomas nodded. 'Looks like drunken, disorderly behaviour to me, Bass.' He pulled his gun and pointed it around the room. 'I'm sure they'll come quietly. They probably need to sleep it off.'

Bishell got shakily to his feet. 'This isn't over, Reeves,' he said. 'This isn't over by a long shot.'

The four men allowed Sheriff Thomas to disarm them then left the saloon at gunpoint, muttering curses as they stepped out into the night.

Bass poured himself another whiskey, left the

money on the bar, and then downed the drink in one sharp swallow. He had no taste for this sort of fighting. His job was to catch criminals, not to take on local yahoos.

Frank entered, frowned at the mess of overturned tables and broken chairs then said, 'Your Injun friend's here, Bass,' he said. 'He's waiting outside for ya.'

Bass nodded. He stepped out into the cool night.

Harjo stood outside, holding the reins of his pinto. He smiled when he saw Bass. 'Looks like you had some trouble in there.'

'Nothing that I couldn't handle. Where's the wagon?'

'I . . . er, thought we could do without the wagon this time,' said Harjo.

'Yeah,' Bass said. 'Good idea.'

They climbed into their saddles then headed along the main drag in silence. Darkness lay over Muskogee, swallowing the town as they left it behind. When they reached the railroad tracks that bordered Indian Territory, Bass had become accustomed to the darkness. He preferred being outdoors, out here in this wild country, to being stuck within four walls. The night air refreshed him and the soft *chirrup* of crickets sounded more melodious to him than anything he had ever heard in a music hall.

The posters, declaring death to any lawman

who dared cross the tracks, fluttered and rustled in the soft night breeze.

Without a word, Bass and Harjo gently urged their horses forward over the deadline.

Nine

'Where do we start?' Harjo asked Bass as they set up camp in the hills.

Bass had considered this since Leo Bennett had told him that Benny had run into Indian Territory. 'We start where we always start John. We ride through the settlements, collecting information. We speak to the Indians. We'll find him.' He unrolled their blankets while Harjo unsaddled the horses.

With the blankets laid out, Bass began constructing a fireplace of stone and mud. Out here, across the deadline, building a fire was a necessity but one which brought danger. Informing others of your location at night was not desirable. Bass brought two long sticks and thrust them into the ground each side of the fire. He draped a blanket across them, far enough away so that they would not be burned, but close enough to shield much of the light the fire would give out.

Satisfied with his work, he spread wood shavings within the fireplace. Bending over them, he used a flint to ignite the kindling. As the flame spread, Bass placed larger twigs over the shavings. The warmth from the fire made him realize how cold the night was.

Harjo came over, carrying two Winchester rifles and a couple of boxes of shells. He lay them on the blankets then sat down. They each took a rifle, checked the working components, and loaded it. Bass preferred the Winchester to his Colts when he was outdoors. The superior range of the weapon, along with its formidable stopping power, had served him well in many firefights.

'You take first watch,' he told Harjo. 'We'll lit out at sunrise, head for Purgatory.'

Purgatory was one of the many settlements that had sprung up in this wild territory. Peopled with thieves and murderers, these rough settlements had been named appropriately; Purgatory, Deadtown, and Hell were among the more lurid names.

Harjo nodded and Bass lay down. He pulled his blankets around him against the night chill and closed his eyes. He kept the Winchester close to hand.

Mist shrouded the trees. Bass walked alone, Winchester in his hands. He looked around for Harjo but the Indian was not here. Walking

66

through the mist, he remembered why he was here.

Benny.

The Winchester felt reassuring in his grip. He knew from its weight that it was fully loaded. Was Benny out here in the misty woods?

He called out 'Benny' several times but the only answer was a cackling of birds. They scattered from the trees, pinwheeling into the air.

Crows.

Scavengers.

Bass watched them closely, watched the patterns their black bodies made as they gyrated through the mist. Perhaps they could tell him where his son was hiding.

A sudden movement to his left caught his eye. Bass spun round, holding the Winchester steady, finger tightening slightly on the trigger. But when he saw the figure standing near the trees, he let the gun's barrel drop.

Benny.

The boy looked different to the smiling, happy youth Bass remembered. Now, Benny looked old beyond his age. A sadness radiated from him in a dark aura. His clothes, a blue shirt and dark pants, were crumpled, loose on his body. He had lost weight and his eyes seemed to stare at Bass from within two hollows.

'Pa,' the boy said. 'Why have you come?'

'To take you, back,' Bass replied.

Benny looked confused. He furrowed his brow, looked into the mist then said, 'Back to what, Pa? My wife is dead. My life is ended. The only thing waiting for me back there is the hangman.'

Bass thought about this for a moment then said, 'Yes, you're right. There's nothing for you.' He lifted the weight of the Winchester, raising the barrel.

Benny looked at the rifle. His eyes widened with fear. 'Pa!'

Bass squeezed the trigger. His son cried out before falling backwards into the darkness.

'Bass, wake up.'

Bass got up fast, dragging the Winchester with him. Harjo crouched next to him, his eyes scanning the tree line. I heard a noise,' the Indian said. 'There's someone out there.'

Bass pumped a round into the chamber of his rifle, shaking his head to dislodge the nightmare. The cool night air brought him to his senses quickly. 'How many?' He peered at the trees but could see nothing in the darkness. He trusted Harjo's senses, though, and knew that if the Seminole said someone was out there, he was right.

'Two, maybe three.'

Bass peered into the blackness, listening for a sound. The fire flickered faintly behind him, sending his own shadow dancing over the trees.

He felt exposed in its light. The rifle felt cold in his hands, but reassuringly heavy.

'There,' Harjo whispered, gesturing toward the trees with his rifle.

Bass squinted, and spotted a shadow moving. He dug his boot heels into the ground then kicked backwards, extinguishing the fire with a bootful of dirt.

The fire died with a hiss. Ghostly starlight illuminated the night.

Bass moved to his right, running in a crouch towards the trees. He knew that Harjo would wait at the camp while he flushed the bushwhackers out. If they both entered the woods, there would be too much danger of shooting each other in the dark.

A noise behind him. Snapping of twigs, rustling of leaves.

Bass spun on his heels, letting off a shot. The Winchester sounded like thunder in the night. More sounds, ahead of him now. A thud. Someone diving for cover. Leaves scattering.

'That was just a warning!' Bass shouted, pumping another shell into the Winchester. 'Come out from where you're hiding.'

He listened.

Chirping of crickets. The soft wind whispering among the trees. His own breathing.

His heart hammered in his chest. He kept his voice level as he shouted out, 'This is Bass Reeves,

US Marshal. If you stay hid in these trees, we'll
flush you out like woodchucks. Give it up.'

'Bass?' The voice in the darkness was familiar.
'That you, Hank?'

'Jeez, Bass, you almost took my beard off with
that shot. It's me and Paul out here.' The leaves
rustled. Bass heard a muttered curse, then Hank
Everson and Paul Rockwell emerged from the
night. Bass breathed a sigh of relief when he saw
the faces of his colleagues.

Everson and Rockwell had been working for
Judge Parker almost as long as Bass. Everson
was a rough character with gnarled hands and
face. At fifty, he was one of Parker's oldest
deputies. Rockwell was one of the youngest. Bass
guessed the boy to be eighteen. His youthful
looks and beardless face belied his talent with a
gun, though. His parents had been killed by a
renegade band of Sioux Indians and Rockwell
had avenged them, even though he had only been
sixteen at the time.

The two stood before Bass, grinning together.
'Woodchucks, huh?' Rockwell asked.

Bass smiled, allowing his body to unwind, his
adrenalin to settle. 'I should have said snakes,
the way you two slither around in the night.
What the hell you doing scaring decent folk like
me and John?'

Everson scratched his grey beard. 'Stakeout,
Bass. There's a cabin over just yonder with the

70

Murphy gang inside. We been on their trail four days. Tracked 'em all the way to this abandoned cabin We saw your fire and thought they'd got a lookout posted. So here we are.'

They walked back to the camp. Harjo began to relight the fire and fix coffee. 'Shows we got a good nose for trouble,' he said to Bass. 'Making camp so close to the Murphys.'

Bass nodded. 'You fellers planning on taking the Murphys alone? From what I hear, they got tempers like wounded coyotes. Noah especially.' Noah Murphy and his brothers Ed and Will were wanted for a number of bank robberies and killings. Judge Parker's men were constantly searching for them in Indian Territory. But until now, the Murphys had been lucky.

'Well,' Everson said, 'now we got you two fellers to give us a hand.'

'All right,' Bass said. 'What you got in mind?'

They drank their coffees around the low fire. Rockwell took a stick and marked out a crude map in the dirt. 'The cabin is sitting opposite some rocks. Hank was gonna wait there with a rifle while I set the Murphys' horses loose. The horses are hitched here.' He indicated an area west of the cabin. 'When they come out to see what all the fuss is, Hank waits until they're all out on the porch then takes a few shots. And we got three dead Murphys for Judge Parker, saving him the trouble of hanging 'em.'

'You sure there's only the three Murphy boys in that cabin?' Bass asked. 'I hear they hire guns for their robberies.'

Rockwell shrugged. 'Well, there may be six of 'em in there all told, judging by their trail. But three or six, what's the difference? Once they're out on that porch exposed—'

'No,' Bass interrupted. 'If there's six men in that cabin, they ain't all gonna come running to see to the horses. Noah Murphy is too cunning for that. He'll send those three hired guns out.'

'Maybe,' Everson said.

'He will. Is there a back way into the cabin?'

'Yeah, there's a back door.'

Bass looked at Rockwell. 'If me and John wait around back, we can break through the door when Hank starts shooting from the rocks. We'll have surprise on our side and the Murphys will likely be watching for trouble from the front.'

Rockwell nodded. 'Sounds good. What do you think, Hank?'

The older marshal stared at the diagram in the dirt then grinned. 'Sure. But you be careful, Bass. That Noah Murphy is sneakier than a rattler. He might try to escape by the back way if he smells trouble.'

Bass drank the last of his coffee. He threw the grounds into the fire then set his cup down. 'It's getting light,' he said. 'We'd best lit out for the cabin.'

72

The four men mounted their horses. Bass slid the Winchester into his saddle boot and checked his twin Colts.

They rode in silence beneath a deep orange sky. Dawn was breaking. For the Murphy gang, it would be the dawn when the law finally caught up with them.

Ten

They reined in near the rocks. Bass slid from the saddle and watched the cabin while the others dismounted. Only a trickle of smoke twisting from the chimney pot revealed that there was life inside the small wooden shack. The windows were dark, the drapes drawn shut.

The horses grazed to the west, within a ramshackle corral. 'If there's six men in there,' Bass said, 'they've been stealing horses. I count ten.'

Everson appeared next to him, carrying a Remington rifle. He looked at the corral then spat. 'Damn horse-thieves.' He shrugged. 'Just one more reason for the judge to swing 'em, I guess.' He took up his position in the rocks, sighting down the barrel of his rifle. 'See any lookouts?'

'No, but the Murphys ain't stupid. There'll be a guard somewhere.' He slapped Everson on the

75

shoulder then returned to the horses where Harjo and Rockwell waited.

'When we get to the back door,' he told Rockwell, 'start setting the horses loose.'

The young deputy nodded then set off towards the corral.

Bass and Harjo skirted the perimeter of the cabin, staying low behind the rocks. They reached the back door as Rockwell reached the horses. Bass slid his Colts from their holsters and held them low at his hips. Harjo positioned himself by the door, ready to break the latch with the butt of his Winchester.

When the commotion came from the corral, it was loud enough to wake the dead. Bass heard Rockwell shout at the horses, then fire his pistol. The animals panicked and stampeded for the gate, which Rockwell had left open. The pounding of their hooves thrummed across the ground.

Grunts came from within the cabin as men were woken by the sound. Bass heard the front door of the cabin being flung open. Three shots rang out from Hank's position in the rocks. Someone in the cabin cursed.

Bass nodded to Harjo. The Indian smashed the butt of his rifle against the latch. The door swung inwards and Bass followed it, guns levelled.

The interior of the cabin was gloomy. Cards and money lay scattered across a table in the centre of the room. Unmade bunks lined the walls. A big bearded man in long johns sat on one of the bunks, rubbing his eyes. He looked at Bass then held up his hands.

At the table sat Noah Murphy. Bass recognized his weasel face from the Wanted posters decorating the courthouse at Fort Smith. Noah seemed unsurprised by Bass's entrance. In his hands, he held a revolver. It was a Smith & Wesson and it was pointed at Bass.

'Drop it, Murphy,' Bass said. Harjo stood behind him, covering the man on the bunk with his rifle.

Noah Murphy looked at Bass, then at the badge on his coat. He smiled shrewdly. 'I've heard of you, mister lawman. US Deputy Marshal Bass Reeves, is that right?'

Bass grunted, his eyes fixed on Murphy's trigger finger.

'Yes,' Noah said. 'I read about you in the newspapers. They say you've never been shot.'

'But I've shot *at* plenty, Murphy. Now drop that iron.'

The outlaw paused, seeming to consider. Then he set the gun down on the table among the cards and crumpled money. 'You must live a charmed life, Reeves.'

Bass took a set of handcuffs from his coat. 'You're the charmed one, Murphy. Your men are dead out there and you're still alive.' He tossed the cuffs on to the table. 'Put those on.'

'Yes,' Noah said, standing. 'Ed and I are so lucky to be safe in here. But have your lawmen friends considered where our brother Will might be?'

Bass backed up to the front door of the cabin, his Colts trained on Noah. 'Paul,' he shouted. 'Will Murphy is out there somewhere.'

Rockwell appeared on the porch, his youthful face dusted with grime. 'Hank took out their hired guns, Bass. You were right about Noah sending them out first.'

'Get in here,' Bass said. 'We missed Will Murphy. He was on lookout.'

Rockwell nodded, looked at the rocks surrounding the cabin, then walked to the door. 'Did you get—'

The shot cut off his speech. Paul Rockwell jerked convulsively, taking two steps to his left. He weaved across the porch like a drunk, staring incredulously at the dark red stain spreading over the front of his shirt. He collapsed into the cabin. Bass grabbed the boy with one arm, struggling to keep the Colt in his other hand pointed at Noah Murphy.

The *crack* of the shot echoed around the rocks then faded. As it disappeared, Paul Rockwell's life went with it. He went limp in Bass's embrace.

Noah Murphy made a play for the gun on the table.

At the same time, Ed Murphy, sitting on the bed, launched himself at Harjo. The Seminole

78

fired but the shot went wild as he fell to the floor in a tangle with the big bearded outlaw.

Bass let off a shot towards Noah. The weight of Paul Rockwell over his arm affected his aim and the bullet slammed into the table, sending a playing card spinning across the room.

Noah snatched up the revolver and fired. Bass fell purposely out on to the porch, letting go of Rockwell's body. Noah's bullet tore a chunk out of the door frame. Bass felt exposed out here beyond the cabin walls. Will Murphy was somewhere in the rocks. 'Hank,' he shouted, 'Will Murphy's out there somewhere. Find him.'

He rolled across the porch then regained his feet as Noah reached the door. The outlaw brought his gun up but Bass was quicker, and firing from a crouching position meant his aim was steadier.

Noah took a bullet in the leg. He cried out and dropped to the porch, clasping his thigh. Bass grabbed the man's gun, tossed it into the dust, then pushed a cocked Colt revolver into the outlaw's face. 'Will Murphy,' he shouted at the rocks, 'I got your brother here. Give it up.'

From the corner of his eye, Bass could see Harjo slapping cuffs on Ed Murphy inside the cabin. The Indian looked breathless but otherwise unharmed. A cut on Murphy's face flowed with blood where Harjo had hit him with the Winchester.

Bass scanned the rocks. He looked down at Noah. 'Tell your brother it's over.'

Noah nodded. 'Will, come on out. They got us fair and square.'

Will Murphy came out of the rocks, Everson behind him. The deputy had his rifle pushed between Murphy's shoulder blades. 'I found him, Bass,' he said. Then he noticed Rockwell's body lying on the porch. His face dropped. 'Paul!'

'He's dead,' Bass said sadly.

Everson brought his rifle up over his head then swung the butt viciously at Will Murphy's head. The outlaw dropped to the dust unconscious.

Everson walked over to Rockwell's body. He slung his rifle away, cradling the boy's head in his arms. 'God damn it! He was so young.' He rocked back and forth slightly, as if comforting the dead deputy. 'We rode together for almost a year.' He started to weep.

Bass hauled Noah to his feet roughly. 'I reckon Judge Parker's got room on his gallows for you and your brothers.' The day was young yet it had already left a sour taste in his mouth. The sun was barely over the horizon and already four men lay dead.

'Hank can take the Murphys and the bodies of their hired guns in his wagon,' he told Harjo. 'I reckon we should bury Paul out here.'

He looked around at the sun-streaked hills and low mountains, at the bright azure sky.

It was as good a place as any for a grave.

The three men stood over the mound of freshly-dug earth, each reflecting on death and the fragility of life. The Murphys were locked inside Everson's wagon along with the bodies of their companions. Bass looked at the mound of earth and the two sticks of wood lashed by leather binding to form a crude cross.

Noah Murphy had been right when he said that Bass had never been shot. He had come close often, having his reins blown out of his hands by bullets, his hat shot off and even his belt cut in two. He had killed a dozen men and knew that his duty would require him to kill more. He knew no remorse, as he had fired in self-defence each time, yet looking at Paul Rockwell's grave made him wonder what it would be like to lose someone close.

What if he lost Benny?

Could he bear to be the one who brought Benny back to the judge, only to get the boy hanged?

The cry of a hawk gyrating in the sky pulled him from his thoughts. He watched the bird's flight. It seemed so free up there, dancing on the winds in the clear sky. Bass turned from the grave. 'We'd best round up those horses the Murphys stole. Someone will be mighty pleased to get them back.'

The horses, which Rockwell had set free from the corral, had returned to the area and stood scattered about in the dust and grass. Bass watched them while Everson and Harjo paid their last respects, then peered closer at a pinto grazing near the cabin. 'God damn,' he muttered beneath his breath.

He pulled a Colt from his holster then strode towards the prison wagon.

Harjo caught sight of him. 'Bass, where are you going?'

'I need to have a word with Noah. Murphy,' Bass said. He reached the prison wagon and threw open the door. The stench of death hit him, as the bodies of the three hired guns lay in there with the Murphy boys. Bass reached in and grabbed Noah by the throat. He thumbed back the Colt's hammer and pressed the barrel of the gun into the outlaw's temple.

'That pinto,' he said angrily. 'Where the hell did you get that horse?'

Eleven

Noah Murphy struggled in Bass's powerful grasp but he didn't answer the question.

'The pinto,' Bass repeated. 'Where did you get it?'

'What's it . . . to you?' Noah asked, gasping for breath.

Bass released his grip slightly. The outlaw took in a deep breath of air. He looked at the pinto. Bass felt himself growing impatient.

'I'll tell you,' Noah said. 'For my freedom. It seems important to you, Reeves. So I tell you and you let me and my brothers go free.'

Bass shook his head, smiling grimly. 'No,' he said. 'You tell me or I blow your head off. Then I ask one of your brothers. If I get no reply, I blow *his* head off. There's three of you, so I got a good chance of getting an answer.'

Noah looked into the lawman's eyes. 'You wouldn't shoot a defenceless man,' he said.

Bass grabbed him and pulled him from the wagon. He twisted Noah's face in the direction of Paul Rockwell's grave. 'That man was a friend of mine,' he said. 'He died because of you and your brothers. Do you think I care if you make it back to Fort Smith dead or alive?'

Noah seemed to consider his position. Bass pressed the Colt harder against his head.

'All right,' the outlaw sad. 'It's only a goddamn nag anyway. Got it at Keouk Falls if I remember rightly. Some black kid owned it. He was getting drunk in the saloon, so we took his horse. Easy.'

Bass knew Keouk Fells by reputation. A saloon town situated in rough land, it was known for its lawlessness and the brutality of its citizens. 'Which saloon?' he asked Noah impatiently.

Noah shrugged. 'I don't remember.'

Bass brought the Colt out of its holster again. 'Which saloon?'

'All right, all right. I think it was called the Devil's Horseman. Yeah, that's it. That kid was so drunk, he must still be sleeping it off.'

'Keouk Falls is two days ride from here. Is that when you saw him? Two days ago?'

'Must be,' Noah said.

Bass hustled the outlaw back into the stinking wagon then shut and locked the door. He strode back to Harjo and Everson at the graveside.

'Benny is in Keouk Falls,' he said. 'At least he was two days ago.'

84

The two men looked confused. 'No wonder you're such a good lawman, Bass,' Everson said. 'I always thought it was down to being a good tracker but now I see you just get these hunches.'

Bass pointed at the pinto. 'That pinto was Benny's. He bought it from Jud Lowe about a year ago. I was with him when he got it. You can still see Jud's brand. The Murphys stole the horse in Keouk Falls. Noah said it belonged to a black kid who was getting drunk.'

Harjo nodded. 'I'll get our things together.' He walked off to the horses.

Everson looked at the prison wagon. 'Well, I guess I'd best get those lousy killers to the judge. They'll hang for sure.' He looked back at Rockwell's grave sadly. 'Bass, this is one of the saddest days of my life. Paul was just a boy.'

'No,' Bass said. 'He was a man. Come on, I'll help you get those stolen horses hitched to your wagon.' He clapped Everson on the shoulder and they walked towards the horses, leaving the grave with its rickety wooden cross behind.

Bass feared for Benny's safety even more now that he knew the boy was in Keouk Falls. He had thought his son might have the sense to avoid the towns in this untamed land. But he knew from past experience that men on the run always sought out other men eventually. He forced himself not to think of Benny lost and alone in that lawless town.

High above, in the cloudless sky, the hawk circled. Then it folded its wings and dropped down towards the alkaline dust, seeking its prey.

Twelve

Keouk Falls had grown like a disease along the small Keouk River. Originally a mining camp, the settlement now housed merchants who catered to the needs of the territory's badmen. Saloons, whorehouses and livery barns stood in jumbled disarray along the main drag. Saloons were predominant.

When Bass and Harjo reached the town, after two days' riding, the sun had started to drop beyond the horizon, staining Keouk Falls a deep blood red. They reined in outside a dilapidated building, which proclaimed itself to be the Manor Hotel, and surveyed the street.

Although it was only dusk, the night's activities had begun. Drunks staggered along the boardwalks, some accompanied by prostitutes. Shots sounded a few streets away, followed by a scream. Men lay in the street, some unconscious, others dead. A bearded man lay outside the hotel

87

in tears, a bottle clutched to his chest like a baby.

Bass untied his saddle-bags and rifle scabbard, throwing them over his shoulder before striding up the creaky wooden steps to the Manor. 'I'll get us a room,' he told Harjo. 'You get the horses watered and fed then meet me inside.'

The Indian nodded. 'You think Benny is still here, Bass?'

Bass looked up and down the street. 'I sure hope not.' He wheeled around then walked past the crying man and into the hotel.

The hotel reception was a small dark room. The drapes had once been cream coloured but were now the dirty brown of ingrained smoke and filth. A rickety staircase led up to the rooms, its dull red carpet threadbare. A man sat behind a scarred desk smoking a large cigar.

'I need a room,' Bass said.

'Yeah, yeah,' the man said. 'A room. We got plenty of those.' He was a fat man with greasy black hair and a beard streaked with grey. His eyes were small and they regarded Bass with open curiosity. 'We got a rule about guns,' he said nodding to the Winchester on Bass's shoulder and the Colts on his hips. 'Gotta leave 'em here.'

Bass nodded. He handed over his weapons. The guns clattered heavily on the desk.

The man handed over a room key. 'Top of the stairs,' he said. 'End of the hallway.' He squirreled Bass's guns into a cabinet behind the desk then locked it with a key hanging from his belt. 'Bathtub is at the other end of the hallway and it costs fifty cents extra.'

Bass handed over the money for the room. 'Friend of mine will be along in a while. Seminole. You can send him up.'

The man shook his head. 'We got a rule about Injuns too.'

Bass sighed. Discrimination had hounded him all his life. In Muskogee and Fort Smith, he was accepted because of his job as a lawman. But he had earned that acceptance through a lifetime of hard work. He had striven to gain something which would have been his by rights if he had been a white man.

He grabbed the man's shirt collar and dragged the man across the desk. 'In the case of my friend, you're gonna break the rules.'

'OK, OK.' The man pulled back, rubbing his neck.

Bass ascended the stairs to his room. It was a small affair with two beds and a single window. The floor was bare boards, the only furniture an old chair and a broken bedside table.

Bass threw his saddle-bags on to the bed then went to the window and pulled back the ragged curtains. The main drag was dark but the saloon windows were lit. Was Benny still here? Was he drinking in one of those saloons?

The trail had been short but already four men

lay dead. The Murphys' hired guns and Paul Rockwell.

Bass drew the curtains across the window, looked at the room with distaste then went down the hallway for a bath. He needed to wash off the trail dust and grime before he headed into town to search for his son.

By the time he got back to the room, feeling refreshed, Harjo was there sitting on the chair. 'I don't think the hotel keeper likes me,' the Indian said. 'He looked at me with a stare that could curdle milk.'

'He'll get used to you,' Bass replied. 'We'll lit out in the morning. By then we should have found out where Benny went, or if he's still here.'

They went downstairs and collected their guns from the desk. The receptionist eyed them coldly as he handed over the weapons. Bass slipped the Colts into the holsters on his belt and realized how naked he had felt without them.

'Do you know where the Devil's Horseman is?' he asked.

The man behind the desk pointed down the street. 'Just past the barber's place. You'll be needing those guns if you go to the Horseman. That place is a heap of trouble. They'll serve anybody in there.' He looked at Harjo with an undisguised look of hatred.

They left the hotel and made their way to the saloon. Raucous laughter and the tinkling of an out-of-tune piano drifted from beyond the batwings. As they entered, the stench of stale smoke hit Bass, underpinned by the smell of stale sweat. The place was full. Men sat at tables playing cards, drinking, arguing, laughing and carousing with women.

Bass and Harjo ordered whiskies. 'You see a black kid in here a couple nights ago?' Bass asked the bartender. 'Came into town riding a pinto.'

The bartender was a tall, skinny man. His clothes seemed to hang from him and his eyes darted about nervously. 'Yeah,' he said. 'I might have seen that kid.'

'A couple weeks ago?' Bass asked.

The bartender shook his head. 'No, this was maybe three, four days ago.'

'That's him.'

'Yeah, the kid was drinking me out of liquor. Ended up sleeping it off in the street then came in complaining the next day that his horse was stolen.'

'You know where he is now?'

'No,' the bartender replied with a shrug. 'We get plenty of men passing through. I don't know the whereabouts of all of 'em. I only remember that kid because he was black. We don't get too many in town.' He looked Bass up and down.

'Did he speak to anyone while he was in here?

Anyone who might know if he left town, or where he was headed?'

The bartender put a hand to his chin. 'I don't know, mister. One night in here's like every other night. I can't remember what happened four days ago.'

Bass gestured around the saloon. 'Any of these men regular customers?'

'Yeah, there's Matt Woollard over there playing cards. He comes in every night. Owns the whore-house down the street and most of the girls in here are from his place.'

Bass looked over at Woollard. The man had short grey-flecked hair and a neat moustache. Dressed in a black waistcoat, black string tie and white shirt with rolled-up sleeves, he sat playing cards with three other men.

Bass walked over. 'Matt Woollard?'

Woollard and the other three looked up from their game. Woollard smiled at Bass but the lawman recognized it as the kind of smile a politician wears before an election. 'Yes, Mr. . . ?'

'My name isn't important. I was wondering if you were in here four nights ago.'

Woollard looked at his cards, then at his companions. 'Yes, I believe we were playing cards then. And I was losing as badly as I am now.'

'Do you remember a young black man getting mighty drunk?'

'Hmmm . . . yes. Yes, I believe I do. The kid

seemed upset about something. But then a lot of men in Keouk Falls are upset about a lot of things.' He looked down at his cards then folded his hand. 'Seems my luck has run dry.'

'Have you seen him in town. since?'

'No.'

'I seen him,' one of Woollard's companions said. 'Kid bought a horse from my barn three days back. Said his pinto got stolen.'

'Did he say where he was headed?'

'West, I reckon. Said he was from Muskogee. Kid seemed to be in trouble of some kind. Well, that ain't strange around here. Still, when those other fellas came asking about him. . . .'

'Other fellas?' Bass asked.

'Yeah. Four of 'em. They were asking around town about the kid.'

'What did they look like?'

'Guy by the name of Bishell was leading 'em. Good-looking man with dark hair. He told me his name when he bought a horse. One of his companions was a big bearded guy, the other two were thinner: one dark, one blond. I thought they was the law, so I didn't say nothing about the kid.'

Bishell. Bass fought to control the anger rising inside him. He had told Bishell to stay put in Muskogee but the fool had taken up the trail.

'Obliged,' Bass said. He turned back to the bar but Matt Woollard stopped him with a touch on the arm.

'One more thing, mister,' he said.

'Yes?'

'If this Bishell is the man I'm thinking of, there's something more you need to know.'

'What's that?'

'Four men were in here two nights back. They sound like the four Jed just described. I saw them talking to Frank Carley. Frank is a regular customer at my establishment but he seems to have left town.'

Bass had heard the name. Carley was wanted for a dozen murders stretching back five years. He was a fast gun and mean with it. He was also said to be an expert tracker. 'You saying Carley has joined Bishell?'

Woollard shrugged. 'It's possible. I can read people better than I can read cards. I think I know who you are by your reputation. Of course, you would never admit to it in this town. Let's just say that I respect justice and that's why I'm giving you the warning about Carley.'

Bass touched his hat. 'Thanks.' He walked back to Harjo. 'Benny has ridden on. Joe Bishell and his men are on the trail too.'

Harjo frowned. 'We must find your son quickly.'

Bass nodded. He thought of the riders tracking Benny through the territory.

'We ride at dawn.'

Thirteen

At noon the following day, they came upon the tracks of riders. Bass dismounted and wiped the sweat from his forehead with a kerchief. The day was hot even though dark clouds scudded across the sky.

He studied the hoof marks in the dust, running his fingers across the imprints. 'Yeah, there's five of 'em,' he told Harjo. 'Looks like Frank Carley is riding with Bishell after all.' He looked at the far horizon. 'If we ride hard, we could maybe catch them by tomorrow.'

Harjo pointed at the far off hills. 'The storm will slow them down.'

Bass pulled himself back up into the saddle. 'Storm, John?'

The Indian nodded. 'They ride into dark clouds. Very dark.'

Bass scratched his stubbly chin. The sky looked overcast, but nothing more. Yet he was used to John Harjo's Indian ways and had relied on them in the past. 'If you say so. How long before we ride into this storm ourselves?'

The Seminole watched the hills. 'A day at most. Bishell and his men will be seeking shelter now.'

'And Benny?' Bass worried that his son knew little of survival in the wilderness.

'Depends how far ahead of Bishell he is. He cannot afford to stop for long.'

'Neither can we,' Bass said. He urged his horse on towards the hills.

Frank Carley brought his horse to a halt. He had been leading Bishell, Stringer and the Block brothers along the trail since dawn and he felt ready to rest. Damn joints weren't what they used to be. He stretched his leg against the stirrups, wincing as pain flared in his knee. He knew from experience what that pain meant. 'Storm's coming,' he said to the others.

Bishell drew up alongside him. 'Storm? What the hell you talking about, Carley?'

'I can feel it in my bones.'

Bishell sighed. 'I hired you to help us find the kid, not to take it easy. We need to keep riding if we're gonna catch him.'

Carley turned in his saddle to face Bishell. The knee pain flashed through his leg. 'I'm tellin' ya, we got to find shelter. The kid'll keep. He won't be going nowhere in a storm.'

Bishell sighed. He looked at the grey sky. 'I

96

don't see no damn storm. I'm paying you good money to track that kid for us, Carley. You gotta earn it. Besides, his pa is on the trail, probably not far behind us. We gotta keep riding.'

'Well, if his pa catches up with us, we outgun him five to one,' Carley sneered. He had only accepted Bishell's money because the job involved Bass Reeves' son. 'That son of a bitch put a friend, Luke Simmons, six feet under.'

'Bass rides with an Injun,' Bishell said. 'And we ain't out here to take up personal grievances. We're here to find the kid. That's what I'm paying you to do.'

'Seems to me your hatred for the kid is a personal grievance.'

'That's different. Benny Reeves is a murderer.'

Carley shrugged. 'Way I see it, so is his pa.'

A light rain started to fall, staining the dust of the trail a dark brown. 'See,' Carley said. 'Storm's starting.' His bones were never wrong. 'There's some old Injun caves about a mile from here. We can wait it out there.'

'I say we ride on,' Bishell said. 'What do you boys say?' He turned in his saddle to face the Block brothers and Ned Stringer.

'I don't want to tangle with Bass Reeves again,' Harry Block said. His brother Al shook his head.

'Me neither.'

'Me neither,' Ned Stringer said, shooting a cursory glance over his shoulder.

'And I say five to two is good odds,' Carley insisted.

'And I'm paying your wages,' Bishell said. 'We ride.'

Carley shrugged. He could bide his time. If they followed the kid, Reeves was sure to follow. Then Simmons' death could be avenged. 'All right,' he said. 'We do it your way. But this storm is gonna slow us down some and make the trail harder to follow.'

'Just follow it, Carley. If we have to deal with Bass Reeves, then we have to. But not if we can avoid it. I want that no-good son of his, and I want to see him swinging on a rope for what he did to Mary Lou.' He spurred his horse on angrily.

Carley sighed to himself. He sat in the saddle, listening to the raindrops rhythmically pattering on his hat brim. Then he rode on, watching the sky and wincing at the pain in his knees.

In the distance, thunder rumbled.

Fourteen

The rain pelted down and thunder thrummed so loudly it vibrated through the earth as Bass and Harjo approached the old Indian caves. Harjo rode point, scanning the cave entrance, Winchester in his hand. Bass took up the rear, similarly armed. He felt the rain soaking through his clothes, chilling him.

'It looks safe,' Harjo said. 'They did not take shelter here.' He slid from his saddle then walked up to the cave mouth.

Bass dismounted. They led the horses into the cave, out of sight. While Harjo busied himself feeding and watering the animals, Bass fixed a fire. As it started to blaze, illuminating the cave walls, Bass stared in surprise. 'You seen these paintings, John?'

Harjo came and sat by the fire. 'I have heard of this place before. My ancestors knew of it.' He pointed to a painting of Indian hunters stalking a buffalo. 'These are their legends.'

Bass peered into the gloom. 'How far do these caves go?'

'For a great distance into the hills.' He removed his hat, followed by his waistcoat and shirt, then his pants. Setting up a framework of sticks, he put the clothes by the fire to dry. Sitting in the firelight, naked except for his longjohns, his muscular torso tattooed with suns, moons and wheels, he looked like an ancient medicine man. Bass was often impressed by the way Harjo had adapted to living in two different cultures. He was a true Westerner, yet his Indian heritage was never forgotten.

Reeves supposed he was similar himself. Although he was now a lawman, he would always be an ex-slave. He could never forget his own heritage.

He removed his own clothes and laid them out near the fire. Steam rose from them as they started to dry. 'You were right about the storm,' he told Harjo.

'Yes.' The Seminole went to his saddle-bag and removed a small leather pouch embroidered with blue beads. 'Let us learn other things.' He emptied the contents of the pouch into his hands then showed them to Bass.

Bones. Tiny animal bones.

Bass had seen Harjo use the bones before. The Indian had a talent for seeing things in the way they spread on the ground. Once, when Bass had been tracking Bill Dosier, Harjo had seen fire in the bone spread. True enough, when Bass finally caught up with the outlaw in Indian Territory, Dosier had set alight the saloon Bass was drinking in before escaping.

'This is a good place,' Harjo said. 'The place of my ancestors. The spirits speak strongly here.' He scattered the bones into the dirt near the fire then bent over them, his face intent as he sought to divine a meaning from their positions.

To Bass, the bones seemed to have no pattern. They looked jumbled, irregular. Yet he respected the Indian ways and knew from experience that they weren't all hokum.

Harjo shook his head slowly, his long black hair seeming to shimmer in the firelight. 'This is not good, Bass.'

Bass felt a tingle creep up his spine. He figured he was letting the atmosphere of the cave get to him. 'What do you see?'

'Death,' the Seminole said. 'The trail we ride is a killing trail. Men's blood will feed the earth.' He looked closer at the scattered bones. 'I see two riders.'

'Is it us?'

'Two dark riders.' Harjo nodded. 'It is us. Now I see only one.'

'What do you mean?'

'Two dark riders become one.'

'What happened to the other one?'

Harjo looked up. In the firelight, his eyes seemed to glow with a supernatural light. 'Death. For one of us.' He looked back at the bones. 'I see a hanged man.'

'Benny.'

'I cannot see his face.'

'Is he dark? Like the riders?'

'Yes.' Harjo grabbed his own throat. 'Tight. Hard to breathe.' He collected the bones with a swoop of his hand and dropped them back into the leather pouch. 'Enough, Bass. The bones will not speak any longer.' He rubbed his neck gingerly as if it hurt him.

'You saw Benny hanged?' Although he had always known of the possibility of such an outcome for his son, hearing Harjo voicing it in this way distressed Bass.

'I saw a hanged man. Maybe not Benny.'

But Bass understood the significance of Harjo's vision. Benny was going to hang. He supposed he had known it all along but hearing it now sent a wave of despair through him. Why did the boy have to be so damned impulsive?

'John, can these things be changed?'

The Indian shook his head. 'The spirits speak strongly here. These things will happen.'

Bass got up and walked past the horses to the cave mouth. Outside, the rain whipped down over the hills, accompanied by bright tongues of lightning and deep peals of thunder. He watched nature's fury, feeling his own build up inside him.

He or Harjo would die and Benny would be hanged.

Four men already dead.

He shook his head. He would not accept it. He respected the Seminole ways but he had to believe that a man created his own destiny. Otherwise, this trail they were riding led only to death.

'I already knew Benny would hang,' he whispered, trying to convince himself.

But he realized for the first time that somewhere, deep inside, he had always aimed to save Benny from the noose. He had thought about taking the boy north to Canada as Jenny had suggested, and releasing him to start a new life. As he had told his wife, though, that made everything he had ever done in the name of justice a lie.

The alternative, to bring his son back to Judge Parker to be hanged, was unbearable.

There is another way.

He looked back into the cave, at his gunbelt lying atop his shirt. The Colts' dark wood grips seemed almost red in the firelight.

He remembered his dream a few nights back. He remembered the question he had asked himself when he had ridden from John and Elly's house. Which was the better death? The gun or the noose?

He watched the storm and realized that he had no idea what he would do when he caught up with Benny. All he knew was that he had to find the boy before Bishell and his lynching party.

And as far as Harjo's bones went, Bass believed that a man carved his own future. Bones be damned.

He felt tired. He watched a streak of lightning fork down from the storm clouds into the hills, then turned from the storm and walked back into the painted cave.

Fifteen

Frank Carley felt wet and miserable. The ache in his bones had disappeared but a biting coldness had replaced it. He sat on a log among a stand of pine, cleaning his revolver and cursing Bishell under his breath. Bishell himself was helping Ned Stringer to remove the saddles from the horses. Al and Harry Block sat opposite Carley, warming their hands at the campfire. The fire did nothing to warm Carley's bones or temper.

'If that idiot had taken shelter when I said, we could be in those caves now, keeping warm, instead of in these damn trees.' He spat into the fire.

Al Block shrugged his huge shoulders. 'Ain't so bad here.'

'Ain't so bad? Ain't so bad you say? We got driven in here by the storm and it's just as wet in these trees as it is on the damn plains. I lived my whole life out here, and I take notice of what Mother Nature tells me. It's the only way to stay alive. That damn boss of yours comes out after this kid and suddenly thinks he's an expert outdoorsman.'

'He ain't our boss,' Al said.

'Well it sure looks like it the way you follow him around.'

'He's the one got the problem with the kid so it's his affair,' Harry said. 'We're just here to help. Joe's helped us in the past, so we're repaying the favour.'

'Chasing some frightened kid all over the Territory? He couldn't do that himself?'

Harry shrugged. 'There's the kid's pa to think about too.'

'Yeah,' Carley nodded. 'I been thinking about him a hell of a lot since Luke Simmons got killed.'

'Nothing to do with us,' Al said. 'I got no quarrel with Bass Reeves.'

Carley picked up a stick and started to poke the fire. 'Yeah? I hear he whipped you boys pretty good back in Muskogee.'

Al looked down at his boots and Harry shrugged, but Carley could see the shame on their faces.

'Look at your friend Bishell over there,' Carley said, nodding towards the horses. 'He's too scared to rest a minute in case Reeves catches up with us. You want to repay a favour to that man, I'd say you could do it best by taking Bass Reeves off his trail for good.'

Al frowned and seemed lost in thought but Harry nodded slowly. 'Maybe you're right. Reeves has got it coming, probably more so than his son. Joe is driven on by the murder of Mary Lou but that don't mean nothing to us.'

'Exactly,' Carley agreed.

'And Reeves does need teaching a lesson for what he did to us in Muskogee.'

'Yep.'

'But we don't want to have a run-in with him again. He's too good with those guns of his. We've heard lots of tales about him.'

'Well,' Carley said, 'tales are one thing, but I got an idea that'll see us safe enough.'

'What you got in mind?' Harry asked.

Carley grinned and threw the stick into the flames. He stood up and pointed back in the direction they had ridden from. 'There's a small bottleneck in the rocks back there. We rode through it about a half-hour ago. I say we wait up in those rocks with our rifles and wait for Reeves and his Injun to come through. Easy. Like shooting prairie dogs, except Reeves and his Injun won't be able to go to ground and hole up.'

Harry nodded but the bear-like Al said, 'What about Joe? He's not gonna want us riding back a ways.'

'I thought you said he wasn't your boss.'

'He ain't but. . . .'

'I told you, it's the best way to help him. Once

107

we get rid of Reeves, we can take all the time we need to get his son.'

Al frowned. He looked to his brother for guidance.

'I think it's a good plan,' Harry said. 'We won't be in no danger up in those rocks.'

The big man nodded. 'All right, I'm in.'

'Good,' Carley said. He looked up through the trees at the darkening sky. 'This storm ain't gonna let up until tomorrow. We camp here tonight then ride back to the rocks in the morning.' He smiled. 'That lawman's gonna get the surprise of his stinking life.'

'Who's gonna tell Joe?' Al asked.

'Leave that to me. I'll tell him and if he doesn't like it, well that's too bad.' With the thought of killing Bass Reeves, the sharp ache in his joints had actually softened to a dull throb. The thought of spending the night in the trees, on the wet ground, depressed him but he focused on tomorrow morning when he could finally avenge Luke Simmons' death. Carley snorted softly. Hell, vengeance didn't mean all that much to him and neither had Luke Simmons.

He just wanted to get a shot at US Deputy Marshal Bass Reeves.

Sixteen

Bass rode through the trees, listening for the sound again. It had floated to him on the soft summer breeze, a whimpering full of anguish.

'Hello?' he called. 'Anyone there?'

He scanned the shadows for movement. The noise wasn't threatening and Bass felt strangely calm as he rode through the trees. He looked down at his gunbelt and discovered that his Colts were missing. His holsters were empty. But even this discovery did not worry him.

He didn't need his guns any more.

He came to a clearing where the sun beat down on deep green grass. In the centre of the clearing he saw Benny. The boy was curled up like a possum playing dead, his knees drawn up to his chest. And he was softly crying.

Bass slid from his saddle and left his horse. Walking over to his son, he felt a sudden fear for the boy's future. He looked so fragile here in the *clearing. So sorry for what he had done.*

'Benny?' Bass said softly.

Benny stopped crying, sniffed, and then looked up. 'Pa?'

Bass went down on his knees and cradled his son's head like a baby's. 'It's OK, Benny. I'm here.'

Benny looked into his father's eyes. 'Have you come to take me back, Pa?'

Bass shook his head. 'No,' he said. 'I've come to take you from the men who are chasing you, away from the badness.'

'I did evil, Pa.' Benny started to cry again.

'I know, son. But that's past now.' He stood up and turned to his horse. 'We're going away.'

They sat in their saddles, the Rocky Mountains stretching off to the north. Bass looked around, not sure how he had got here. But that didn't matter now. All that mattered was Benny. He turned to his son.

'You ride, boy. Follow the Rockies north and don't stop until you reach Canada.'

Benny nodded. 'Thanks, Pa.' He reached out and they embraced tightly. Then the boy spurred his horse north, riding into a new future.

Bass watched for a while, then turned his horse around. As he turned into the sun, a glint of metal from the front of his coat caught his eye, dazzling him.

Sunlight reflecting from his badge.

*

Bass sat up in his blankets, startled awake. He looked around the cave but could see nothing except the Indian paintings on the wall. The fire's orange glow cast eerie shadows over the rocks. He dressed quickly, fastened his gunbelt to his waist then walked to the mouth of the cave.

Harjo stood outside, his Winchester held loosely in his hands. Dawn was still a couple of hours away but already threads of orange laced the clouds.

'You didn't wake me,' Bass said. 'It was my turn to stand watch an hour ago.'

Harjo shrugged. 'I could not sleep in the cave. The spirits brought me dreams.'

'Dreams?'

'Of the future, maybe.'

Bass shrugged it off then went to see to the horses. The day looked like it was going to be a fine one. A little cool, but dry underfoot. Good riding weather.

He saddled up the horses, whistling a low tune to himself. He felt refreshed after his sleep, cheerful even. He wondered if the dream had made him feel this way.

A dream of the future?

He ran his fingers over the cold metal of his marshal's badge. He thought about the men he had trailed, captured and brought before Judge

Parker. He remembered the twelve men he had killed. He'd had no choice; they had fought to the death rather than face the 'Hanging Judge'.

Would Benny give himself up? Did he have any less to lose than those twelve men?

Bass continued to cinch the saddles on the horses.

And he didn't whistle any more.

Seventeen

Frank Carley woke up early. Tie rain had stopped during the night and the ache in his bones had dulled, but he had hardly slept. He took some dry clothes from his saddle-bag and changed quickly in the cool morning air. He looked around the camp at the other sleeping men, noticing that Joe Bishell's bed was empty. He looked around the trees and spotted the missing man sitting on a log some distance from the camp. He walked over.

'Bishell, we need to talk.'

Bishell stood to face Carley and it was obvious that he had been crying. His eyes were red and puffy.

'You OK?' Carley asked.

Bishell nodded. 'I will be when we catch that son of a bitch and string him up for what he did to Mary Lou.'

'Listen, me and the Block boys are gonna ride back a ways and get his pa off our trail.'

113

'Don't be stupid, Carley.'

'We can take him at the bottleneck in the rocks. Him and his Injun friend. Give us more time to find the kid without worrying about the law on our tail.'

Bishell sneered. 'What makes you think you can take out Bass Reeves when so many others have tried and failed?'

'He's just a man,' Carley replied. 'And in my experience, a bullet will stop a man every time.'

'I hired you to help me find the kid. We got no deal if you go back.'

Carley shrugged. 'Then you can keep your money. I got no quarrel with some kid who killed his wife. She probably deserved it if she was seeing you behind his back.'

'Why, you—' Bishell sprang forward, his hands going for Carley's throat. The attack surprised Carley but his lightning-fast reflexes brought his forearms up, blocking Bishell's grip. He brought his elbow up sharply. It connected with Bishell's chin, sending the man stumbling backwards.

Before Bishell could regain his senses, Carley whipped his gun out. He pointed it threateningly. 'I told you how it's going to be, Bishell. You ride on after that kid if you want but me and the Blocks are going back for Reeves.'

Bishell wiped blood from his lips with his shirt. He stood up straight, looking Carley in the eyes. 'All right, you go back. But don't let me see you again because next time I do, the first thing you'll know about it will be the feel of a bullet in you.'

'You talk big,' Carley said, 'but you ain't even wearing your gunbelt.' He spat on the ground then turned and walked back to the camp. He had never liked Bishell anyway. The Block brothers and Ned Stringer were awake, roused by the argument. Carley looked at Al and Harry. 'Let's go shoot us a prairie dog,' he said.

Harry climbed out of his blankets but the bear-like Al remained where he was.

'You coming?' Harry asked his brother.

Al shook his head. 'I been thinking about it and I don't see why I should risk my neck. We came out here to help Joe find the kid. Killing Bass Reeves wasn't part of the deal.'

Harry looked at Carley then at his brother. Carley had known all along that it was Harry who was more enthusiastic about getting Reeves. There was a meanness in his eyes that said killing excited him.

'You coming?' Carley asked.

Harry nodded and began to get dressed. 'Way I see it,' he said, 'that lawman's got it coming anyway. Hell, we'll be heroes in these parts if we take out Bass Reeves.'

Carley smiled. He had been thinking the same himself. The name of Bass Reeves was a name feared by every outlaw in the Territory. If he and

Harry Block could remove that fear, they would become Oklahoma legends.

Joe Bishell, Ned Stringer and Al Block watched him with disdain from the camp as he hefted his saddle on to his horse and began fixing the buckles and straps. He didn't care. In fact, he felt good. The sun was shining and the ache in his bones was gone.

He checked the Remington rifle in its scabbard.

As he dismantled and cleaned the weapon, he whistled a nameless cowboy folk tune.

Today was going to be a good day.

Eighteen

Bass and Harjo rode west, following the trail of the five riders. The grassland through which they rode smelled fresh after the storm. The air felt cleaner, invigorating. The sky was a deep blue, the sun high and hot. The coolness of the morning was gone.

Bass let his thoughts roam. He wondered how Jenny was coping. He knew that her distress would be doubled by the fact that she didn't know what was happening to either her son or husband. At least he was out here, close behind Benny, and not sitting in the house worrying.

He watched the trail ahead closely. He was sure they were getting closer to Bishell and his men. In the distance, the grasslands gave way to a cluster of high rocky hills. To the south stood a small stand of trees through which a creek ran. Bass slowed his horse then brought it to a stop. Harjo did the same.

'I reckon we should water the horses at the creek,' Bass said. He wiped the sweat from his forehead with his kerchief.

Harjo nodded and spurred his horse towards the trees.

As they reached the shade of the pine, the air turned cooler. They dismounted and Harjo led the horses to the creek while Bass lit his pipe.

He sat on a rock, tamping tobacco into the pipe bowl and listening to the sounds of birds singing and the slight wind whispering through the pine. He reckoned this was the best place to work, out here in the untamed wilderness. He thought of Marshal Leo Bennett stuck behind a desk at Fort Smith all day. Bass knew he would get cabin fever if he ever had to work indoors, shut off from nature and all her wonders.

He lit the pipe, sucking on it gently. The smoke tasted smooth in his throat, the breeze cool on his face.

Harjo came back with two tin mugs of water. He passed one to Bass. The liquid was cold and clean.

'I think we are close,' the Indian said.

'Yeah, I think so too.'

'We will soon be taking Benny back home.'

'To the judge, you mean.' Bass picked up a rock. He weighed it in his hand then tossed it into the creek. It splashed noisily, disturbing the birds. They fluttered in the trees before resettling.

'Bass, have I ever told you the story of Moki-Waka?'

'No, but I get the feeling you're going to.'

Harjo smiled then nodded. 'Moki-Waka was a tribal warrior. He was respected in his village and he had a beautiful wife named Suki. Moki-Waka was a great huntsman and all his life he had heard a legend that a great wolf with one pale blue eye roamed the forest near the village. Men called this wolf "Ghost Eye". Many had tried to kill Ghost Eye to prove themselves but none had succeeded. Moki-Waka told the elders that he would go into the forest alone, then find Ghost Eye and kill him. This would prove that he was the greatest huntsman of all.'

'Brave man,' Bass said puffing on his pipe. He had heard some of Harjo's stories before and knew that the Indian only told them when he had a point to make.

'Yes, he was a brave warrior. He left the village for many weeks and searched the forest for Ghost Eye. He killed many wolves but none of them had one pale blue eye. Moki-Waka became homesick but he dared not return to the village until he had succeeded in his quest. Weeks turned into months and still he did not see Ghost Eye. And as time passed, he missed his wife and his village more and more.

'Finally, he could not stand to be alone in the forest any longer. He gathered up all the wolf

119

skins that he had collected and he sewed them together to form one large pelt. Then he found a small round stone near a river and used berries to stain it blue. He returned to the village claiming that he had killed Ghost Eye and that the wolf's eye had turned into a blue pebble upon its death.'

Bass chuckled. The Indian stories always had a fairy-tale quality about them, but he wondered if they weren't grounded in some fact. He knew much of the Indian ways and he knew how they could weave legendary stories from a series of mundane events.

'Moki-Waka was hailed as a hero,' Harjo continued. 'The tribe proclaimed to others that their warrior had killed Ghost Eye. A year went past and Moki-Waka enjoyed the admiration of his people, but inside he felt a dark guilt about what he had done.

'After a year, though, a hunting party from a neighbouring tribe came to the village. They were celebrating because they had killed a great wolf in the forest. The village elders asked to see the wolf and when they did, they felt ashamed. The wolf had one blue eye.

'Moki-Waka was branded a liar and outcast from the tribe. He was told that he should live in the forest alone for the rest of his days. This he did, leaving his beautiful wife behind.'

The Indian fell silent. Bass said, 'So what are you trying to tell me, John?'

Harjo looked across the creek. 'Moki-Waka realized that he had done wrong and he willingly accepted his punishment. I believe your son will do the same. You are worried that he will resist arrest?'

Bass nodded. 'Yes.'

'From what I know of Benny,' the Seminole said, 'he is a good young man. You brought him up to know the ways of honour and righteousness. He has done wrong and in his panic he fled, but I believe he will return to Fort Smith with us willingly.'

Bass hefted another stone into the creek. 'And if he doesn't?'

'Then you will know what to do.'

Bass extinguished his pipe then knocked the burnt ash out on to a rock. 'John, I've killed twelve men in my career as a lawman. Sometimes, when I'm alone or almost asleep on the trail, I think about those men. I remember all their names. I don't want to add Benny's name to that list.'

'Benny will come quietly, Bass.'

'Will he?' Bass stood up, stretched his limbs then looked at the hills to the West. 'Well, I guess we'll find out soon enough. We'd best get back on the trail.'

They mounted their refreshed horses then rode hard towards the hills.

Nineteen

'Two riders coming!' Harry Block shouted to Frank Carley.

'I see 'em,' Carley shouted back. 'We wait until they're right below us before we start shooting, right?'

'OK.'

Carley peered over the rocks and saw the dust rising in the distance. It had to be Reeves and his Injun. He could just make out two dark forms in the dust. They were riding hard towards the ambush. He grinned to himself. In a couple of minutes, he would be a hero among the outlaws of this Territory.

He would be known as the man who shot Bass Reeves. He broke open a box of shells and levered one into his Remington rifle. He scattered the others in the dirt at his feet, close to hand.

Crouched as he was behind the rocks, he had a steady, solid, aiming position. He rested the Remington's barrel on the rocks, sighting along

123

its length. His knees hurt from crouching but he ignored the pain. 'You ready, Harry?' he called.

'Yeah, I'm ready.'

'You take the Injun and I'll take Reeves.'

'All right.'

Carley waited as the shapes in the distance got closer. He could hear the horses' hoofs pounding the dust. Not long now. He wondered which of the riders was Reeves then realized that he must be the big one on the left. He had heard about Reeves's powerful build. He moved the rifle sight to track that rider.

'Just a little closer, you son of a bitch,' he whispered.

He could clearly see the dark faces of the riders now. The Injun's long hair streamed behind him as he rode. Reeves looked stronger and more solidly built than Carley had imagined. The black Deputy Marshal's face had a determined look about it and Carley could almost see why this man's exploits were modern-day legends.

He couldn't wait any longer. He had a good, clear shot. One pull of the trigger would put him in the history books. He adjusted his position slightly, half-standing to get even more of his target into his sights.

A sharp pain stabbed into his right knee. Carley grimaced in agony as his leg gave way. He collapsed behind the rocks, squeezing off a shot as he fell.

As he lay cursing his arthritic joints and hastily reloading his rifle, he wondered if his shot had met its target and if Bass Reeves was dead.

The sound of the shot brought Bass from his thoughts about Benny. He had been pondering the question of whether or not Benny would give himself up when the *crack* reached his ears. The next thing he knew, he and his horse were tumbling to the dust. He wondered if he had been hit. He felt no pain but had heard that sometimes men were shot and dead before they even realized it.

As he hit the ground, though, he realized it was his horse that was dead. The animal buckled beneath him, sliding into the dirt. Bass kicked out against the stirrups, throwing himself clear of the fourteen-hundred-pound carcass. He hit the ground hard, crying out as he felt his left shoulder wrench painfully backwards. He rolled in the dirt with the momentum of his fall, seeing nothing but the sky and the dusty ground spinning round and round in his vision.

Finally, he came to a stop in a cloud of dust. With his right hand, he whipped out his Colt pistol. His left arm felt numb so he left the gun's twin in its holster. Keeping low, he ran for the cover of some scrub to his left. Only seconds had passed since the shot and Bass waited for a second.

As he reached the scrub, it came. The shot echoed around the rocks. Harjo, who had been trying to slow his horse after seeing Bass fall, suddenly tumbled backwards out of his saddle. He landed heavily in the dirt.

Bass shouted, 'John!'

The Indian lay silent in the dust.

Cursing, Bass squinted against the sun. He could see nothing but the hills covered with scree.

He raised his head higher, then dropped it as two shots rang out from the rocks. One bullet tore up the dirt near his hand. He lay still, breathing heavily and ignoring the pain in his left shoulder. He felt like a trapped rabbit; there were at least two shooters up in those rocks and he didn't know if Harjo was alive or dead.

Two riders become one.

Bass forced the Indian's prophecy out of his head. He had no time to dwell on it now. He cursed himself for riding towards such an obvious place for an ambush; he should have scouted ahead first.

Peering around the scrub at Harjo's motionless body, he shouted, 'John, can you hear me?'

No answer.

Bass's horse lay dead twenty yards from his hiding place. Too far to attempt to reach the Winchester in the saddle boot. He would need the rifle to stand a chance against the gunmen in the

126

rocks; the range was too great for his pistols.

Harjo's pinto sauntered about the trail, throwing its head and rolling its eyes with confusion. The shots had unnerved it and it had lost its rider. It moved in a circle, unsure of its intended direction.

Bass whistled to get the animal's attention. One long, low note.

The horse stopped. It snuffled and shook its head.

'Here,' Bass said in a soothing voice. 'Over here, boy.' He had known horses all his life and he knew that as a herd animal, they required a leader. An animal like Harjo's pinto would treat a human as that leader. It was part of the process by which horses were broken and domesticated.

'Come on,' Bass called.

The horse looked in his direction then slowly trotted towards him, its head bobbing up and down. When it reached him, Bass took the reins and brought the horse's head down so that he could stroke its muzzle. 'Good boy,' he whispered. Staying low, he slid along the ground until he lay beneath the left stirrup. Above him, in the saddle boot, was Harjo's Winchester.

Bass was sure that his own horse had been shot accidentally, that the shot had been intended for him. No man who lived out in the West would shoot a horse; they were much too valuable a resource. Even horse theft was a major crime. With this in mind, Bass crouched behind the horse, shielded from the rocks by its girth. He holstered his Colt then slipped his left foot into the stirrup and grabbed the saddle horn with his right hand. He used the strength in his arm to lift his body clear of the ground. With his right boot tip he nudged the pinto's rump, guiding it forward.

The horse trotted towards the rocks. Bass kicked harder. He needed speed for what he was attempting.

The pinto picked up its pace to a canter. Bass clung to the saddle, ignoring the burning pain in his muscles. He knew his plan was crazy but he had no better ideas.

Just as he got near the rocks and thought he was going to make it, he heard a shot. The pinto skewed sideways then dropped to the ground, dead.

Bass grabbed the Winchester as he dropped to the dirt.

Frank Carley lay against the rocks in a position that afforded him a view of the trail below, but also relieved the pain in his knees. He cursed his luck. His shot had killed Reeves' horse and the marshal had escaped into the scrub bushes. At least the damn Injun was dead.

Carley popped a shell into the Remington then

scanned the scrub where Reeves was hiding. 'We got him now,' he shouted to Harry.

Reeves's head appeared over the bush and both men fired. Carley quickly reloaded his rifle. He grinned to himself. The deputy marshal had no chance stuck out there in the scrub.

When the pinto moved over to Reeves' position and then trotted towards the rocks, Carley frowned. The bastard was using the horse as cover. 'We can't let him get close,' he shouted to Harry. 'Shoot the damn horse.'

'I ain't shooting no horse,' came the reply from the rocks across the bottleneck.

'Damn it!' Carley raised his rifle, tracked the pinto then let off a shot. He hated wasting a good animal like that but he couldn't afford to let Reeves get any closer.

Horse and rider fell heavily to the ground. Harry Block stood up to get a better look. 'Jeez, Carley, you didn't have to do that.'

'Get down, you idiot!' Carley dropped behind the cover of the rocks. He had seen Reeves grab the rifle from the pinto's saddle.

But his warning to Harry Block was too late – Bass Reeves had already begun firing.

Bass spotted the two men among the rocks and fired too hastily. His bullet ricocheted around the hills. Levering another shell into the chamber, he shot again. His target cried out then fell forward, his body tumbling heavily over the rocks. Bass

129

adjusted his aim but the other man was gone.

Climbing to his feet, Bass ran forward to the rocks, keeping his body low to offer less of a target. He guessed that the man who had dropped out of sight would be on the run, but he couldn't be sure that he wasn't just taking cover and waiting.

He reached the rocks safely but he still felt wary. Then the sound of galloping hoofs from beyond the bottleneck confirmed his suspicion the man was running. Bass sprinted along the trail in time to see a rider hightailing it into the distance.

He cursed then turned and ran back the way he had come. He needed to see to Harjo. He prayed his friend wasn't dead.

Two riders become one.

Damn bones.

Harjo lay on his back, blood seeping from a ragged hole in his chest. Bass knelt down, placing a hand on the Indian's chest. He could feel a heartbeat, regular and strong. He let out a breath of relief.

Sprinting to his dead horse's body, Bass opened the saddle-bag and found his bandages, knife and iodine. He carried medical equipment every time he rode, although he had never required it for himself.

He returned to Harjo then knelt and inspected the bullet wound. He was thankful that the

Indian was unconscious because what he had to do next would be painful.

He took the knife and gently prodded the soft flesh around the wound. He regretted the fact that he didn't have the time to light a fire and sterilize the knife. Steadying his hand, he pushed the blade in, feeling for the bullet. The tip of the blade hit hard metal. Bass twisted the knife then pulled the tip upwards. The bullet appeared at the entrance of the wound and he flicked it away into the dust.

He took the iodine and uncapped the bottle before pouring a little into the wound. Harjo stirred, groaning.

Bass bandaged the wound quickly, wrapping the bandage around the Indian's shoulder to keep it in place. There was nothing more he could do, nowhere he could take his friend. Both horses were dead.

He would have to set up camp until Harjo recovered. And Bishell's men and Carley would get closer and closer to Benny.

Bass cursed but realized he had no choice. Then he spotted something on his backtrail which worried him further.

Riders.

Twenty

There were four of them. Bass stood with the Winchester held loosely in his hands. As the riders approached, he recognized their leader. Matt Woollard, the whorehouse owner from Keouk Falls. Bass relaxed the grip on his rifle slightly.

Woollard and his men brought their mounts to a halt. Dressed in a plain blue shirt and wearing a hat and boots, Woollard looked different from the poker-playing businessman Bass had met in Keouk Falls. 'Your friend still alive?' Woollard asked, nodding at Harjo's prone body.

Bass nodded. 'He needs a doctor.'

Woollard dismounted. 'Bill, Pete, get this man on his horse and take him back to Doc Foley.'

'Our horses are dead,' Bass said.

Woollard scratched his chin as if considering. 'All right, we'll make a litter for him. There's plenty of trees around. Henry, ride back to Keouk

133

Falls and fetch us a couple more horses. Bill and Pete, get to work on that litter.'

As the men got to work on their tasks, Woollard turned to Bass. 'You can take my horse and a couple of my men.'

'I appreciate your help, Woollard, but why are you doing this for me?'

Woollard smiled. 'Amazing thing, the telegraph. As I told you when we first met, I thought I knew who you were. Well, we got news today that US Deputy Marshal Bass Reeves's son murdered his wife and is on the run in the Territory. His father is on the trail. I got my men together and we're here to help. We may live in Keouk Falls, Mr Reeves, but some of us still respect law and justice.'

'I appreciate it,' Bass said. 'And I'd appreciate the loan of your horse. But as for your men, I can't ask anyone to ride this trail with me. It's my job, I'm wearing the badge, and that means I have to do it. You take your men back to Keouk Falls.'

'There's five vigilantes standing between you and your son. I think you need all the help you can get to see that justice is done and that some lynch mob doesn't take the law into their own hands.'

Bass shook his head. 'There's four. One of 'em is lying dead in the rocks over there.'

'But four against one. . . .'

'I ride alone,' Bass said. 'I don't want anyone else getting hurt.'

'Mr Reeves, you see those men cutting wood to make a litter for your Indian friend?' Woollard gestured to the men he had ordered into the trees. They were both stocky and muscular, both dark.

'I see 'em,' Bass said.

'That's Bill and Pete Johnson. Maybe you've heard of them.'

Bass nodded. 'I heard of the Johnson brothers. They were part of a posse a couple years back. Helped Sheriff Bob Anderson catch the Walker gang. Pete Johnson killed Ed Walker.'

'That's right. So you see, my men are no strangers to danger. I told them what is at stake and they volunteered to come out here with me to lend a hand.'

Bass considered his position. It was true that he needed all the help he could get now that Harjo was wounded. Alone, he didnt stand much chance against four gunmen. 'All right,' he said to Woollard, 'I accept your offer. But we're a horse short.'

Woollard nodded, deep in thought. 'Bill can stay here and look after your friend. Henry will be back soon with fresh horses and then they can take the Indian back to Keouk Falls. Pete can ride with us and you can take Bill's horse. That makes it three against four, not good odds but better than you going it alone.'

Bass nodded in agreement. 'As soon as that litter is done, we need to ride.'

'Bill can finish the litter while he waits for Henry to get back. Soon as you trade your saddle for Bill's, we can get on the trail and find your son.'

By the time Bass had cinched his own saddle to Bill Johnson's horse, Harjo was awake. He lay covered in blankets although the afternoon was warm. Bass knew that shock chilled a man.

He walked over to his injured friend and laid a gentle hand on his shoulder. 'How you doing, John?'

Harjo attempted a weak smile but his face looked drawn. 'Not well. I am dying, Bass.'

Bass shook his head although he had seen dying men before and recognized the signs in Harjo's shallow breathing and pinched features. 'You're going to see the doctor in Keouk Falls.'

'No,' Harjo said calmly. 'I will be making a different journey, a journey to the Great Spirit.'

Bass felt a great sadness weigh down on his body. He had known Harjo for years, had ridden the trail with him and considered him a great friend. To see his friend dying now beneath a blanket in outlaw territory was unbearable. Elly would never cope with her husband's death, Bass knew, and he would have to tell her what had happened. She had been against John coming with Bass from the beginning, and now Bass wished he could turn back the clock to that moment on their farm. But it was too late.

'Bass, I want you to bury me here. Mark my grave with the eagle talisman from my saddle-bag.'

Bass nodded sadly. 'Perhaps one day, I'll bring Elly out here to see it.'

Harjo attempted a smile but winced with pain. 'I shall not be here, my friend. My spirit will soar with the hawks. Tell Elly that I have always loved her.'

'I will, John.' Bass felt his throat constrict and for the first time in his life, he felt like he might shed tears. He had been brought up to keep his feelings hidden and the lessons of a hard life had made him a hard man, but watching John Harjo die undid all that learning. He felt a salty tear slide down his cheek.

The tear fell from his face and landed on Harjo's blanket. Bass noticed that the blanket no longer moved with the rise and fall of the Indian's breathing.

John Harjo was dead.

Standing over the Seminole Indian's grave, Bass swore a silent oath that someone would pay for his friend's death. Woollard and his men kept a respectful distance while Bass placed the circular metal talisman bearing the image of an eagle on to the freshly-turned earth. He had dug the grave himself while Bill and Pete Johnson, abandoning the construction of the litter, had retrieved the body (which turned out to be Harry Block) from the rocks and buried it in a shallow grave some distance away.

Bass turned to them. His desire to find Bishell and his men now burned through every part of his body. 'Let's ride,' he said.

Woollard and Pete Johnson saddled up and Bass took one last look at John Harjo's grave before climbing into his own saddle. The day was fading into dusk and in the sky a hawk cried out, riding the winds on its great outstretched wings as it hunted its prey.

Bill Johnson wished them luck, then the three men rode for the bottleneck between the rocks.

Bass was aware of the time they had lost here and knew that they would have to ride damn hard to catch up with Bishell before Bishell caught up with Benny.

The three riders spurred their horses along the trail as darkness fell. The clock was ticking.

Twenty-One

Joe Bishell slowed his horse as he spotted the buildings in the distance. He raised his hand and Ned Stringer and Al Block, who had been riding behind him, brought their mounts to a stop beside his.

Joe pointed ahead. 'Anyone know what those buildings are?'

'Yeah,' Stringer said. 'Used to be a town called Heartbreak. When the silver mines ran dry, it became a ghost town. A good place to spend the night.'

'That's what I was thinking,' Bishell said. He pointed to a dilapidated stable on the main drag. 'Looks like we finally reached the end of the line.' A horse stood in the stable.

'Goddamnit,' Stringer said. 'The kid's here.'

Bishell nodded. 'OK, we gotta play this nice and easy to make sure he doesn't run. He could

139

be in any of those buildings. I suggest we split up and flush him out.'

They rode to an old hitching rail and secured their horses before moving in separate directions along the main street, guns drawn.

Bishell limped to an abandoned saloon. His left leg stung him as he walked, but the bullet that Bass Reeves had put into it had passed cleanly through and the doctor had said that as long as Bishell rested, it would heal fine. Well, he couldn't afford to rest as long as Mary Lou's killer was on the loose.

He kicked his way through the old batwings and entered the saloon. The dust in the place almost choked him. It lay in a thick carpet on the wooden floor. It was undisturbed, so Bishell guessed the Reeves kid hadn't been in here. He turned and walked along the rickety boardwalk to the next building.

The door was missing. He strode through into an abandoned hotel. A jumble of broken furniture lay on the floor. And on the stairs, a set of footprints in the dust led up to the first floor.

Got you, you murdering bastard.

He walked across to the foot of the stairs and peered up into the gloom. He knew from the state of the old wooden steps that if he set foot on them, they would creak and give him away. So he would have to move fast to catch his prey.

But he couldn't move fast up the stairs because

of his bad leg. He cursed under his breath and walked to the doorway.

The night was getting darker, the stars bright pinpricks in the blackness. Bishell spotted Stringer and Block across the drag and waved them over. They moved silently across to him.

'Kid's up the stairs,' Bishell whispered. 'You gotta move fast and get him.'

They nodded in unison and made for the stairs. Stringer sprinted up to the first floor with the bigger Block behind. Bishell heard doors being kicked open, then shouts.

After a moment, Block came down, with a struggling Benny Reeves held in his hands. Reeves's hands were pinned behind him by Block's massive paws and the kid looked scared. Real scared.

Bishell had never seen Mary Lou's husband before. His clandestine meetings with her had always been away from Muskogee and he had never seen the Reeves kid in town. He thought the kid looked too innocent to be a murderer. His face, streaming with tears, was just a boy's and his frame was slight.

No, he told himself, not a boy. A murderer.

'Well, Reeves, we caught you,' he said. 'And we're gonna make you pay for what you did to poor Mary Lou.' At the thought of Mary Lou, Bishell felt a surge of anger. He brought his hand hard across the kid's face.

Reeves cried out as he received the blow then started to moan, 'I didn't mean it. I didn't mean to do it.'

'Shut up!' Bishell shouted. He slapped the kid again and Reeves shut up.

'Al, there's some rope in my saddle-bag to tie him with. I want plenty of light to see this son of a bitch swing, so we'll hang him at dawn. We'll take turns guarding him tonight.'

Al nodded then dragged Reeves into the street. Stringer followed, covering the kid with his gun.

Bishell smiled to himself. Finally, he would be able to avenge Mary Lou's death. He wondered briefly if the kid's pa might still be on the trail then dismissed the thought.

Carley and Harry must have taken care of Bass Reeves at the rocks. They were probably riding all over the Territory by now, telling their story to anyone who would listen.

Killing a man to elevate one's personal status was something with which Joe Bishell did not agree. Killing a man who had murdered his wife was something else again, though. Mary Lou had been so lovely. Bishell knew he would miss her for the rest of his life. At least he had a chance to make things better by hanging her killer.

It wouldn't be long until dawn. He needed to get some rest; the ride had been long and hard and his wounds hurt him.

He turned his back on the abandoned hotel

and walked across the main street of the ghost town. Tomorrow, he would add another ghost to its population.

Twenty-Two

Frank Carley knew the ghost town of Heartbreak well; he had holed up there a number of times when on the run from the law. He chuckled when he realized that Bishell's trail led to the abandoned town. A ghost town was a good place for a killing.

Wherever Bishell went, Bass Reeves would follow. And when Bass Reeves arrived, Frank would be waiting.

He dismounted just beyond the outskirts of Heartbreak and led his horse through the night towards the buildings. He spotted four horses in the old stable and realized Bishell must have caught the kid. He wondered if young Reeves was swinging yet or if Bishell would wait until morning before hanging him. No matter either way.

Frank led his horse behind the buildings across from the stable. At the rear of the hotel, he found a patch of grass good enough for his horse to graze on. He hitched the animal there, out of sight, then removed his saddle and slung it over his shoulders. He approached the hotel's back door and listened for a while. The place sounded empty.

He shouldered the door open and entered the dark building. Navigating by touch, he made his way through the broken furniture to the stairs, which he ascended. He found a room with a musty old bed and a window that overlooked the main drag.

He dropped his saddle on the floor then placed the Remington rifle and a box of shells on the windowsill. This was the way Bass Reeves would enter town and, when he did, Frank would be ready.

He settled down on the bed and removed his hat. He had a few hours until dawn and could afford a quick sleep. Despite the dust and dilapidated condition of the room, he knew he would sleep well tonight. After all, he had tomorrow to look forward to.

Tomorrow he would become a hero. The man who killed Bass Reeves.

'Mr Reeves, we have to stop a while, give the horses chance to rest,' Woollard shouted.

Bass knew he had pushed his mount to the point of exhaustion by the way the animal trembled as it ran. He slowed the pace to a gentle trot and patted the horse's neck. 'Easy, boy.'

Woollard and Johnson rode up beside Bass. Woollard scanned the dark landscape. 'Pete, are we near Heartbreak?'

Johnson shrugged.

'Yeah, we are,' Bass said. 'I've thought for a while that the trail might lead there. A man on the run usually goes for a town, even a ghost town.'

'Makes sense,' Woollard agreed. 'How long before we get there?'

'Depends on the horses,' Bass said. 'We'll probably reach Heartbreak by dawn.' He had a sense of urgency but knew that they could not push the horses beyond their limits. His keen intuition told him that this trail was coming to an end. He would soon find Benny.

Alive?

Did it matter since he would be taking him back to Judge Parker, who had hanged more men than any other judge?

Maybe it did matter because maybe Benny wouldn't face the judge. Once Woollard and Johnson returned to Keouk Falls, Bass would be alone with his son. They could ride north to Canada. . . .

He pushed the thought away. He was here to perform his duty, to arrest Benny and bring him to justice. He had no other choice if his life as a lawman meant anything at all. But he knew that

147

during the ride back to Fort Smith, he would be tempted to let Benny go free.

He decided not to think about it now. He wasn't even sure his boy was alive.

The three men rode in silence for the rest of the night, each thinking his own thoughts as riders often do during long hours in the saddle.

The dead town of Heartbreak came into view just as the sun began to stain the sky a blood red.

Twenty-Three

Dawn broke over the ghost town. Frank Carley had been awake for an hour, sitting on the bed smoking, watching the main drag. He heard a noise from a building across the way and hunkered down below the windowsill as he saw Bishell walking out on to the old boardwalk.

Frank peered down on to the drag. Bishell, Al Block and Ned Stringer had the Reeves kid and were leading him, hands tied behind his back, down the street. Bishell was carrying a noose. They stopped outside a saloon then Bishell threw the noose up and over the saloon's sign, which had faded beyond all recognition. Bishell pulled on the rope, testing it, then tied one end to a hitching rail in the street.

Frank watched but he had little interest in the kid. As far as he was concerned, the boy had been unlucky enough to get caught so he had to pay the price. These were tough times.

Then something caught his attention that *did* interest him. Beyond the stable, a cloud of dust rose into the dawn sky. It was obviously Bass Reeves but the dust was too much to be made by one rider. And where had the deputy marshal got a horse so quickly?

It didn't matter. Frank had heard about Bass Reeves' resourcefulness and that was why, even though the lawman had been horseless, Frank had fled the scene at the rocks.

He grinned. Alone or with friends, Bass Reeves was about to die. He picked up the Remington, broke open the box of shells and arranged them in a line across the windowsill. He was taking no chances. Sitting on the bed so that his joints couldn't betray him again, he targeted the riders approaching town.

Time to be a hero.

Bishell found a box and placed it beneath the noose. He looked at Benny Reeves then gestured to the box. 'Stand on it.'

The boy was crying quietly but seemed resigned to his fate. Hands tied behind his back, he had trouble climbing on to the box. Al Block picked him up and set him there.

'Al, get that rope around his neck.'

Al pulled the noose down over the boy's head, tightening the big knot behind his neck.

'You got anything to say?' Bishell asked Reeves.

150

'I didn't mean to do it,' the kid cried out. 'It was an accident, I swear!'

'Save your whining. You killed Mary Lou because you didn't want her seeing me. Well now you're gonna pay for her death.' Bishell strode forward to the box.

A shot rang out from the old hotel across the street. Block, Stringer and Bishell dived for cover. But before Bishell did so, he kicked the box out from under the kid's feet.

Benny Reeves dropped, the noose strangling the life out of him.

Bass heard the shot then felt his reins being sliced in two by a bullet. They were approaching the main drag now and Bass could see his son hanging by his neck, kicking with his feet as the last of his life drained away.

'*No!*' Bass shouted. He unleathered the Winchester and brought it up, letting off a shot. His target had been the rope. He was an expert shot and knew that his chances of hitting such a small target at such a distance were fair. But the movement of the horse beneath him spoiled his aim and he missed.

A second shot came, humming from the hotel across the drag and took Bass's hat off. He ignored the threat. He had no time to spare. Pushing himself from the stirrups, he leapt from the horse and landed in the street. He rolled with the momentum then came up into a crouch. Forcing himself to steady his aim, he sighted the rope then fired.

Benny fell flailing to the boardwalk.

Bass turned to the window of the hotel and let off a covering shot then sprinted across to the hotel's door. Woollard and Johnson rode on down the street and Bass heard shots as he entered the hotel's cluttered reception area. He bounded up the stairs, guessing at the door which would lead to the room where the sniper was hidden.

He kicked the door open and entered the room. Empty.

Cursing, Bass turned around and came face to face with a man he recognized as Frank Carley from a number of drawings on Wanted posters.

'Wrong room,' Carley said. He brought a pistol out from his gunbelt and fired.

When Bishell saw the Reeves kid fall to the boardwalk, he felt rage explode inside him. He had come all this way to hang the boy and he wasn't going to be denied his opportunity now. One way or another, Benny Reeves had to die.

Two riders galloped up the street, pistols drawn. Ignoring them, Bishell took his own pistol from its holster and walked over to Reeves. He pointed the gun at the boy's face.

'Time to die,' he said.

Before he could pull the trigger, he felt hot lead

enter his chest, the force of the shot spinning him around. The town seemed to cartwheel in his vision, then became still as he dropped to the boardwalk.

He stared at the dawn sky as he died.

Bass whipped the butt of his rifle at Carley's face. The outlaw's shot went drilling into the floor-boards.

Carley fell backward into the banister that bordered the landing. The old wood splintered and Carley plummeted out of sight. He landed with a loud crash below.

Bass descended the stairs two at a time, Winchester ready in case the outlaw was still in a fighting mood, although he doubted it. A fall like that could kill a man.

Carley lay on the floor amid splinters of wood, still breathing but unconscious. His rifle lay some distance away, out of reach. Bass took the hand-cuffs from his belt, cuffed Carley's hands to a stout-looking post, then went out into the street to find out if his son was still alive.

Twenty-Four

Bass walked over to the old saloon where Woollard and Johnson were busy tying up Al Block and Ned Stringer with Bishell's rope. They had untied Benny. The boy sat on the boardwalk, shivering and sitting on his hands. Bass felt a flood of warmth when he saw the boy. Whatever Benny had done, Bass's love for him was unconditional.

Benny saw him then stood. 'Pa!' He came running across the drag, arms outstretched. Bass caught him up in an embrace.

'Thank God you're all right.'

The boy started crying. 'They were going to hang me, Pa. I told 'em I didn't mean to do what I did. I told 'em.'

Woollard and Johnson came over. 'We had to kill one of 'em,' Woollard said, 'but we did what we came here to do. We got your boy.'

'I'm mighty obliged to you both,' Bass said. 'Frank Carley's in the old hotel. He's still breathing. I'll take him back to Fort Smith with me. He's

155

a known outlaw so he'll hang for sure.'

'We'll ride with you as far as Keouk Falls,' Woollard said.

Bass nodded. He went to his saddle-bag and found three sets of spare handcuffs. He tossed two to Woollard. 'Get these on Stringer and Block.'

He turned to Benny. 'Put your hands behind your back, son.'

Benny didn't protest. He turned around and Bass cuffed him.

At Keouk Falls, Woollard, Johnson and Bass shook hands. 'Good riding with you,' Woollard said.

'Yeah, it was an honour,' Pete Johnson said. He held the reins of his brother's horse. Bass had switched to Bishell's pinto at Heartbreak.

'I'm obliged for the help,' Bass said.

The two men rode towards their home, leaving Bass with the four prisoners, their horses tied to his. 'All right,' Bass said, turning to face them. 'You boys ready to face the judge?'

He felt proud as his son nodded affirmation. It reminded Bass of the story John Harjo had told him about the Indian brave willing to accept his punishment.

Bass knew that there might be a hangman waiting for Benny at Fort Smith but he had to take the boy to meet his fate.

The tin star on his chest wouldn't let him do it any other way.

Author's Afterword

Benny Reeves was sentenced to life in the federal prison at Leavenworth, Kansas, but was later paroled for good behaviour and because of a petition from local residents demanding his release.

Bass continued to serve justice in the Indian Territory, arresting over 3,000 men and killing fourteen. His policy was that he did not shoot until the outlaw he was chasing began shooting first. Despite having his hat brim shot off, his belt shot in two, a button shot off his shirt and his horse's reins shot out of his hands, Bass was never wounded.

Bass was sixty-nine years old when Oklahoma became a state and the Territory ceased to exist. Rather than hang up his guns, he became a policeman in Muskogee. There was not one single crime ever reported on his beat.

Bass retired when he contracted Brights disease, and this, coupled with other ailments, caused his death in 1910, at the age of seventy-two.

The *Muskogee Phoenix* wrote the following account of Bass's life on Thursday, 13 January 1910:

In the history of the early days of Eastern Oklahoma the name of Bass Reeves has a place in the front rank among those who cleansed out the old Indian Territory of outlaws and desperadoes. No story of the conflict of government's officers with those outlaws, which ended only a few years ago with the rapid filling up of the territory with people, can be complete without mention of the Negro who died yesterday.

For thirty-two years, beginning way back in the seventies and ending in 1907, Bass Reeves was a deputy United States marshal. During that time he was sent to arrest some of the most degperate characters that ever infested Indian Territory and endangered life and peace in its borders. And he got his man as often as any of the deputies. At times he was unable to get them alive and so in the course of his long service he killed fourteen men. But Bass Reeves always said that he never shot a man when it was not necessary for him to do so in the discharge of his duty to save his own life.

Reeves was an Arkansan and in his early days was a slave. He became a deputy marshal long before a court was established in Indian Territory and served under the marshal at Fort Smith. Then when people started to come into Indian Territoiy and a marshal was appointed with headquarters in Muskosee, he was sent over here.

Reeves served under seven United States marshals and all of them were more than satisfied with his services. Everybody who came in contact with the Negro deputy in an official capacity had a great deal of respect for him, and at the court house in Muskogee one can hear stories of his devotion to duty, his unflinching courage and his many thrilling experiences, and although he could not write or read he always took receipts and had his accounts in good shape.

Undoubtedly the act which best typifies the man and which at least shows his devotion to duty, was the arrest of his son. A warrant for the arrest of the younger Reeves, who was charged with murder of his wife, had been issued. Marshal Bennett said that perhaps another deputy had better be sent to arrest him. Bass, with a devotion of duty equalling that of the old Roman, Brutus, whose great-est claim on fame has been that the love for his son could not sway him from justice, said, 'Give me the writ.' and went out and arrested his son, brought him into court and upon

159

trial and conviction he was sentenced to imprisonment and is still serving the sentence.

On Saturday, 15 January 1910, the *Muskogee Phoenix* said this:

Bass is dead. He was buried with high honours, and his name will be recorded in the archives of the court as a faithful servant of the law and a brave officer. And it was fitting that such recognition was bestowed upon this man.

It is fitting that, black or white, our people have the manhood to recognize character and faithfulness to duty. And it is lamentable that we as white people must go to this poor, simple old Negro to learn a lesson in courage, honesty and faithfulness to official duty.

As far as lawmen of the Old West go, Bass Reeves ranked among the top ten.

His story is one of courage and devotion.

He will not be forgotten.